PHILIP ALLAN
LITERATURE GUIDE
FOR A-LEVEL

GREAT EXPECTATIONS
CHARLES DICKENS

Marian Cox

Series editor: Nicola Onyett

PHILIP ALLAN
UPDATES

Philip Allan Updates, an imprint of Hodder Education, an Hachette UK company, Market Place, Deddington, Oxfordshire OX15 0SE

Orders

Bookpoint Ltd, 130 Milton Park, Abingdon, Oxfordshire OX14 4SB

tel: 01235 827827

fax: 01235 400401

e-mail: education@bookpoint.co.uk

Lines are open 9.00 a.m.–5.00 p.m., Monday to Saturday, with a 24-hour message answering service. You can also order through the Philip Allan Updates website: www.philipallan.co.uk

© Marian Cox 2011

ISBN 978-1-4441-2162-9

First printed 2011

Impression number 5 4 3 2 1

Year 2015 2014 2013 2012 2011

Printed in Spain

Hachette UK's policy is to use papers that are natural, renewable and recyclable products and made from wood grown in sustainable forests. The logging and manufacturing processes are expected to conform to the environmental regulations of the country of origin.

Cover photo © pixelcarpenter/Fotolia

P01867

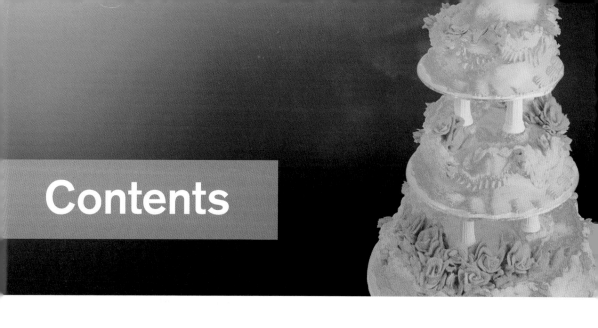

Contents

Using this guide

Why read this guide?

The purposes of this A-level Literature Guide are to enable you to organise your thoughts and responses to the text, deepen your understanding of key features and aspects and help you to address the particular requirements of examination questions and coursework tasks in order to obtain the best possible grade. It will also prove useful to those of you writing a coursework piece on the text as it provides a number of summaries, lists, analyses and references to help with the content and construction of the assignment.

Note that teachers and examiners are seeking above all else evidence of an *informed personal response to the text*. A guide such as this can help you to understand the text and form your own opinions, and it can suggest areas to think about, but it cannot replace your own ideas and responses as an informed and autonomous reader.

Most of the references to the text are to chapters not pages, so that any edition of the novel can be used. Page references for the Top ten quotations refer to the 1996 Penguin Classics edition (2003 reprint).

How to make the most of this guide

You may find it useful to read sections of this guide when you need them, rather than reading it from start to finish. For example, you may find it helpful to read the *Contexts* section before you start reading the text, or to read the *Scene summaries and commentaries* section in conjunction with the text — whether to back up your first reading of it at school or college or to help you revise. The sections relating to the Assessment Objectives will be especially useful in the weeks leading up to the exam.

Key elements

Look at the Context boxes to find interesting facts that are relevant to the text.

Context

Be exam-ready

Broaden your thinking about the text by answering the questions in the **Pause for thought** boxes. These help you to consider your own opinions in order to develop your skills of criticism and analysis.

*Pause for **Thought***

Build critical skills

Taking it further boxes suggest poems, films, etc. that provide further background or illuminating parallels to the text.

Taking it **Further** ▶

Where to find out more

Use the **Task** boxes to develop your understanding of the text and test your knowledge of it. Answers for some of the tasks are given online, and do not forget to look online for further self-tests on the text.

Task

Test yourself

Follow up cross references to the **Top ten quotations** (see pages 89–91), where each quotation is accompanied by a commentary that shows why it is important.

◀ Top ten *quotation*

Know your text

Don't forget to go online: **www.philipallan.co.uk/literatureguidesonline** where you can find masses of additional resources **free**, including interactive questions, podcasts, exam answers and a glossary.

Synopsis

Pip is an orphan being brought up by his much older sister and her husband, the village blacksmith, Joe Gargery. They live at the forge in a village on the Kent marshes. One Christmas Eve he is caught in the churchyard by an escaped convict from the prison ship moored in the estuary. He is threatened and forced to return next morning with food and a file he steals from home. The convict is recaptured by soldiers while fighting with another escapee.

A year later Pip is invited, through Joe's uncle Mr Pumblechook, to 'play' at the gloomy and decaying house in town of an eccentric lady, Miss Havisham, who was jilted on her wedding day years before and has since become a recluse in Satis House. Pip becomes enamoured of her beautiful but cruel ward, Estella, whom Miss Havisham adopted and raised to exact revenge upon the male sex.

At the age of 14 Pip is apprenticed to his brother-in-law, but he dreams of becoming a gentleman and being able to marry Estella. He confides this dream to Biddy, the young woman who comes to work as housekeeper at the forge after Pip's sister is crippled and made dumb by being hit with a convict's leg-iron. Pip suspects that her attacker was Orlick, the surly forge employee who is jealous of Pip.

Four years later, Pip learns from a visiting London lawyer called Jaggers that he has 'great expectations' and is to be turned into a gentleman. Pip assumes that Miss Havisham is his mysterious benefactor and that he is intended for Estella. This knowledge makes him dismissive of Biddy and the devoted Joe, and he is glad to leave them and set out for London.

> Pip learns from a visiting London lawyer…that he has 'great expectations'

Pip goes to the capital to be educated and taught manners by Herbert Pocket and his father, who are relatives of Miss Havisham. He shares rooms with Herbert in Barnard's Inn and befriends Wemmick, the clerk in Mr Jaggers's office near Newgate Prison, whom he visits in his home in Walworth which Wemmick shares with his aged father. Pip lives an unhappy and idle life in London, getting himself into debt. He is snubbed by Estella. He is ashamed of Joe when he comes to London to visit him. Pip goes to Satis House occasionally, but he avoids visiting the forge and does not go home until the occasion of his sister's funeral.

On reaching the age of 21, Pip receives £500 and uses some of the money secretly to buy Herbert a partnership in a shipping firm. He is jealous of Estella's encouragement of a disagreeable young man called

Bentley Drummle, and is dismayed by her coldness towards Miss Havisham.

When he is 23, his true benefactor appears one stormy night; it is none other than Abel Magwitch, the marsh convict, who became rich from sheep-farming after being transported to Australia, and who never forgot Pip's charity. After his initial horror at the revelation of the low source of his expectations, Pip gradually overcomes his aversion and tries to save Magwitch, alias Provis, from the death penalty he has incurred by returning to England. Magwitch is in danger from his former fellow convict, Compeyson, who was the jilter of Miss Havisham and the man he was fighting with on the marshes. Pip learns that Estella is to be married to Drummle, and all his hopes now crumble.

Pip goes to Satis House to take leave of Miss Havisham before accompanying Magwitch abroad. She asks for forgiveness and then her dress catches fire; she dies soon afterwards, despite Pip's attempt to save her. Pip is tricked by Orlick, working for Compeyson, into meeting him at the sluice-house on the marshes, and he is nearly murdered before being rescued by Herbert.

Compeyson overturns the boat taking Magwitch to a steamer moored at the mouth of the Thames and dies in the water, while Magwitch is seriously injured. Pip informs Magwitch, before he dies in prison, that Estella is Magwitch's daughter. Joe comes to London to nurse Pip through a long and dangerous illness. When Pip recovers, he resolves to cast off his social pretensions and marry Biddy, but finds when he goes to the forge that he has left it too late, as she has just married Joe.

Pip joins Herbert in business in Egypt, lives with him and his new wife Clara, and prospers, finally making a gentleman of himself through his own efforts. On his return to England, 11 years later, he meets the now-widowed Estella by chance at the derelict Satis House, and 'saw the shadow of no parting from her'.

❮ Top *ten quotation*

Chapter summaries and commentaries

Volume I

Chapter 1

At the age of seven, Pip is seized by an escaped convict in the village graveyard in which his parents and siblings are buried. Pip is ordered to bring food and a file from the blacksmith's where he lives, under threat that a fellow convict will otherwise find Pip and eat him.

Commentary: **This Gothic opening shows the world through an imaginative child's eyes, mixing humour and horror. Pip is presented as the unprotected orphan of fairytale, setting up the expectation that he will be preyed upon by wicked adults. He and his world are turned upside down. Iron (represented by the file and the black lines of the scenery, which connote prison bars) and food become recurring motifs in the novel. The equation of animate and inanimate — the gravestones with the people under them — is typical of Dickens's descriptive technique, as is the use of extended similes: there are three 'as if' constructions in this chapter. Crime, guilt and death are introduced as themes (with the convict, the graveyard and the gibbet on which a pirate died). Dickens's use of detail for either comic or sinister effect is shown in the unnecessary naming of Pip's five dead brothers. The convict, like Joe Gargery, is given comic spelling, e.g. 'pecooliar', to show his low class. The bleak setting is that of the Kent marshes beside the Thames estuary, where Dickens spent his early childhood, and many of Pip's fears and preoccupations were his own.**

Context

See 'Biographical context' for details of Dickens's life (p. 60 of this guide).

Chapter 2

Pip's sister punishes him for being late home, and also bullies her husband Joe. Pip has nightmares before getting up early on Christmas morning to take brandy and a pie from the pantry, and a file from the forge, to the convict.

Commentary: **Mrs Joe is a domestic tyrant, a wicked stepmother figure. She does not use her first name and is associated with metallic, wound-inflicting instruments symptomatic of her lack of maternal feeling and harsh actions. Her husband is the opposite, a gentle giant presented as a helpless child. Mrs Joe is both farcical and disturbing as a guardian, as this domestic environment of casual violence, unjust punishment and suppression of imagination is the one in which Pip is growing up. The ironic Christmas nativity for Pip is the birth into his life of the convict, who has made him into a thief. Dickens's style often relies on triple paratactic structures and there is an example here with the repetition of 'I was in mortal terror'.**

paratactic

juxtaposition of clauses or phrases without the use of conjunctions

Chapter 3

Pip comes across the other convict on the misty marshes before making his rendezvous with the first, who gobbles his food and begins freeing himself from his leg-iron, with the intention of finding his companion.

Commentary: **The fear, pity and guilt of the child are conveyed through the naive narrator. The mist is a symbol, used later in the novel, for moral perplexity and emotional turmoil. Because the other convict does really exist, even though he sounded fictitious because exaggerated, it is difficult for Pip — and the reader — to separate reality and fantasy, a problem which will pursue him throughout the novel. The intrusion of the criminal world into routine home life has been set up in this chapter, the two being connected by the food and file, the threats of adults and Pip's guilty conscience.**

Context

Dickens had a lifelong interest in the law and justice, and especially capital punishment. For another sympathetic response, read the novelist William Makepeace Thackeray's article 'Going to see a man hanged', available at www.exclassics. com/newgate/courv. htm

Chapter 4

The Hubbles, Mr Wopsle and Mr Pumblechook (Joe's uncle) come to Christmas dinner, which is uncomfortable for Pip because he is bullied by Pumblechook, and is afraid that his theft will be discovered. When

Dickens played an important role in 'inventing' the idealised concept of 'the Victorian Christmas' especially through his short story *A Christmas Carol.* You might wish to read this classic text and compare Dickens's presentation of the perfect family Christmas at the end of this story with the Christmas setting of *Great Expectations.*

Context

Because many classic Victorian novels were serially published in monthly magazines, they often feature dramatic climaxes and cliffhanger endings, rather like modern soap operas. The first instalment of *Great Expectations* was published in the Christmas edition of Dickens's magazine *All the Year Round* in 1860 and instalments followed every month until August 1861.

Task 1

How does Dickens establish the child's viewpoint in the first five chapters?

it is, he runs for the door and into a group of soldiers, one of whom is carrying a pair of handcuffs.

Commentary: **This travesty of a Christmas dinner, where Pip is abused and given unpleasant food to eat, has its comic moments but reaches its fearful climax with Pip assuming the handcuffs are for him, his criminalised self who lost his innocence on Christmas Day, before going to church. Pumblechook's silly name is an indication that he is a buffoon, but one with the power to inflict pain on Pip. It is fitting that he should drink Mrs Joe's medicinal tar-water as a punishment, and that Pip should have been the one to put it into the brandy. The convict is further linked to the forge by the discovery of the theft, the handcuffs for Joe to mend and the interruption of Christmas dinner on his account.**

These early chapters were published in December 1862, making the Christmas setting chronologically as well as thematically appropriate. There is an example of authorial voice in the comment that 'Cleanliness is next to Godliness, and some people do the same by their religion.' 'Naterally wicious' is an example of misspelling to create comic effect, as well as being a reference to the Victorian belief that children were guilty of original sin.

Chapter 5

When Joe has fixed the handcuffs, Wopsle, Joe and Pip follow the soldiers on their search for the convicts and find the two men fighting. Pip is anxious that his convict, who has prevented the escape of the other, does not believe that he led the soldiers to him. Pip's convict admits to the thefts from the forge, thus saving Pip from punishment.

Commentary: **This is a scene of 'the survival of the fittest', and it foreshadows later struggles between these two men, who are representatives of different social classes. It is because Pip is capable of compassion for the 'poor wretches' that he is aligned with the charitable Joe, as distinct from all the others present. This ability to feel pity, even for those who have wronged him, will later be the saving grace of the snob that the adult Pip becomes. This chapter contains one of many passages in the novel where firelight is contrasted to darkness (the forge, Satis House, the sluice-house), a motif evocative of the traditional description of hell.**

Chapter 6

Pip does not feel able to confide in Joe about what really happened with the convict. Pumblechook and Wopsle argue pointlessly about the convict's putative method of entry into the pantry.

Commentary: **From now on Pip will drift apart from Joe because of his guilty secret. The construction 'if Joe knew it' is used three times to stress the emotional tension of Pip's decision not to tell him. The adult narrative voice condemns Pip for being cowardly at this time. The juxtaposition of comedy with the pathos of the end of the previous chapter ('as if it were all over with him') is typical of the way in which Dickens manipulates and alternates the reader's mood. There is, as there often is in the novel, a passing reference to hanging in this chapter, but in a comic context.**

Chapter 7

We learn that Joe is illiterate, Pip's education is limited and that Joe married Pip's sister only to help with Pip's upbringing. Mrs Joe and Pumblechook return from market and announce that the rich and reclusive Miss Havisham wants a boy to go and play at her house in town. Pip is sent to her, escorted by Pumblechook.

Commentary: **This is a pivotal plot point and the beginning of expectations for the child seemingly destined to become a blacksmith's apprentice. It is another step away from the goodness of Joe, and the innocence of his country childhood, that Pip has started to patronise Joe. Pip's literal interpretation of words is a device for capturing the child's viewpoint at the beginning of this chapter. Village education and the Wopsle family are satirised; Biddy is introduced as a fellow victim and orphan. Joe's performance with the poker is another metal image, this time purely comic — unlike that of Mrs Joe's wedding ring being scraped over Pip's face. The theme of gratitude is stressed.**

Pip visits Satis House and meets Miss Havisham, in the David Lean film version of 1946

AF archive/Alamy

At Satis House, Estella turns away Pumblechook and takes Pip to meet the extraordinary broken-hearted woman in her decaying room. When they play cards, Estella mocks Pip for his coarseness of appearance and speech; this upsets Pip, which pleases Estella.

Commentary: **The Gothic urban upper-class decay and self-indulgence of Satis House is another new world to Pip, but there are links with the convict episode in the bleakness of the environment, the giving of food and the image of hanging. Pip is now the poor and despised creature, the 'beggar', that Magwitch seemed to him. The premises include a disused brewery, a symbol of failed conviviality with a taint of decadence.**

Estella, the star in the darkness with a lighted candle…

Estella, the star in the darkness with a lighted candle, is the 'queen' or fairytale princess of the castle, with a locked gate to represent the iron bars surrounding her heart. Miss Havisham, the travesty of a bride with her looking-glass, is the witch figure who is also compared to an inanimate waxwork and a corpse. There is a clue to her connection with Compeyson in the touching of her heart (the other convict had allegedly threatened to cut out and eat Pip's heart, but it will be Miss Havisham who causes it to break). Pip's hallucination of the dead Miss Havisham foreshadows her demise, but also her haunting of his life while still alive.

Chapter 9

Pip fabricates a fantastic account of his visit to Miss Havisham on his return to the forge and is gently reprimanded for lying by Joe.

Commentary: **Pip has decided to keep Satis House separate and secret from his real life, which will lead to problems later. His imagination has been given free reign and has carried him away, making him unable to gauge the truth in relation to either Estella or Miss Havisham; he has transferred his loyalty to them, afraid that they would be misunderstood by common folk. The gold, silver, coaches and velvet of his story are attributes of fairytales; the four dogs are the 'four little white crockery poodles on the mantelshelf' (Chapter 4) of the forge, transformed by Pip's grandiose imaginings.**

The chapter ends with an image of the forging of a first link of a binding chain.

Chapter 10

Coming home from his useless evening school, Pip finds Joe and Wopsle in the village inn with a stranger, who has Joe's stolen file and who gives him two pound notes.

Commentary: **The criminal world of London has reached out and found Pip in his village, and his guilty secret is resurrected. The stranger who gives him money and knows Magwitch is a clue to the source of Pip's future expectations. The appearance of mysterious strangers is a fairytale device and a feature of detective novels.**

Chapter 11

On Miss Havisham's birthday, and anniversary of her being jilted, her relatives gather at Satis House in the hope of being left something in her will. Pip meets Jaggers, not knowing who he is. Miss Havisham shows Pip the wedding table on which she will lie when she is dead, among the spiders and mouldy cake. Pip meets a boy with whom he reluctantly has a fight, which delights Estella enough to reward Pip with a teasing kiss.

Commentary: **'The Witch of the place' enjoys tormenting her relations, the 'toadies and humbugs', as much as she does Pip. The 'pale young gentleman', who is a relative of Miss Havisham, will further foster Pip's delusion, when he gets to London and meets Herbert again, that Miss Havisham is his benefactor. The decaying, mice-eaten 'bride-cake' is another food symbol, this time of the ravages and ironic reversals of time which conflates human and object so that Miss Havisham can say that they have come to feast upon her, and that 'sharper teeth than teeth of mice have gnawed at me', using cannibalistic images reminiscent of the opening chapter. The descriptions of the relatives, and even the insects, are comically detailed, despite the sombreness of the place and the occasion. Estella, like all romance heroines, likes the idea of men duelling for her favours.**

Estella likes the idea of men duelling for her favours.

Chapter 12

Pip continues to visit Satis House to 'play' for nearly a year. Mrs Joe and Pumblechook look forward to Pip being rewarded; Pip tells Biddy he

Context

See 'Social and cultural contexts' (p. 64 of this guide) for more about apprenticeships.

looks forward to leaving the forge. However, Miss Havisham asks to see Joe so that Pip's apprenticeship to him as a blacksmith can be arranged.

Commentary: **Once again Pip is plunged into guilt about something that was not his fault: the fight with Herbert, in which the latter is the loser. Mrs Joe and Pip have their expectations dashed, and this foreshadows and mirrors the later revelation that Miss Havisham is not his benefactor.**

Chapter 13

Joe accompanies Pip to receive money from Miss Havisham for Pip's apprenticeship, and the indentures are signed. Pip does not feel there is any cause for celebration at the Blue Boar inn, although his sister is happy to receive the 25 guineas.

Commentary: **The comic interview with Joe prefigures his appearance in London in his Sunday best, where he is equally uncomfortable. The recurring images of law and punishment are evoked with references to Pip now being 'bound' to Joe. Pip's disappointment is conveyed by his scathing descriptions of Pumblechook in ever more derogatory terms as 'detested seedsman', 'fearful imposter', 'abject hypocrite', 'basest of swindlers', 'diabolical corn-chandler'. He is now old enough to see through this hypocritical relative, but not able to correctly judge other adults, benevolent and malevolent.**

Chapter 14

Pip has to buckle down to work in the forge, hiding from Joe his dissatisfaction with this 'coarse and common' existence.

Commentary: **The chapter begins with a sententious statement in the authorial voice that becomes Pip's. The flat, low, featureless marshes are used as a pathetic fallacy for Pip's mood and prospects without Estella.**

Chapter 15

Pip is determined to pay another visit to Satis House. His co-worker at the forge, Orlick, demands a half-day holiday too, and this leads to a fight between him and Joe, giving Mrs Joe hysterics. Pip finds that Estella

Context

Young women from high society were sent to Europe at the end of their education to be trained in cultural and social accomplishments (such as French dancing and etiquette), to prepare them for their future lives as wives and hostesses.

has been sent abroad to be 'finished' as a lady. He agrees to visit Miss Havisham every year on his birthday. After meeting Pip in town, Wopsle puts on a performance concerning someone who went off the rails and murdered his uncle, and Pip is made to feel guilty by Pumblechook about this fiction. Returning to the village, Pip and Wopsle come across Orlick behaving furtively and hear the guns signalling the escape of a convict. On arriving home, Pip finds that Mrs Joe has been attacked and crippled by a blow to the head.

Commentary: **Joe was right, as he often is in his simple, intuitive way, to warn Pip against going to Satis House on the grounds that no good could come of it, as Pip is now even more unhappy to know that Estella is no longer there. There is here another fight with a female spectator who gets very excited. Once again there is an escaped convict on the loose. Mrs Joe's injury, rendering her speechless, is poetic justice. Pip, used by Orlick as an alibi, is mired in the criminality and brutality of the marshes and the forge. The scene in the forge is depicted as a climax of a play, with a body on the stage and an audience. There will be another tragi-comic performance by Wopsle (Chapter 31). That Wopsle is an actor enhances the theatrical motif, and draws attention to the further levels of fiction and fantasy within the fictional construct of a novel presented as a factual autobiography.**

> The scene in the forge is depicted as a climax of a play

Chapter 16

Pip now feels guilty about his sister, especially as he believes that the assault weapon was Magwitch's leg-iron. Police fail to solve the crime. Mrs Joe signals that she wants Orlick brought to her, and is strangely pleased to see him. Biddy comes to live at the forge as housekeeper, since Mrs Joe is now incapacitated.

Commentary: **Mrs Joe and Orlick are bonded by a crime, as perpetrator and victim, in a similarly macabre way to that of Pip and Magwitch. The leg-iron, which Pip provided the file for the removal of, is an image of both metal and criminality, and of person turned into object; it is like a ghost which haunts Pip.**

Chapter 17

Still torn between his work at the forge and his annual visits to Satis House, Pip confides in Biddy that he wants to be a gentleman and

explains his reason. She advises him to forget Estella. Orlick follows them home from their walk on the marshes.

Commentary: **Pip associates Estella with the picturesque aspects of the landscape, showing how he has idealised her. His fantasies, self-pity and jealousy of Orlick indicate his confusion about his feelings for Biddy, the obvious person he should be considering as a marriage partner, but whom he patronises. Orlick appears from the 'ooze' — a type of horror image — and is thus a creature of the mud like Magwitch.**

Context

See the section on Mary Shelley's *Frankenstein* in 'Literary context' (p. 69 of this guide).

Chapter 18

Four years into Pip's apprenticeship, Jaggers enters the Jolly Bargemen, where Wopsle is holding forth about a murder trial, and asserts himself. He goes home with Pip and asks Joe to release Pip from his apprenticeship because a secret benefactor is offering him 'great expectations': Pip must go to London to be educated to become a gentleman, with Matthew Pocket as his tutor. Joe and Biddy are upset.

Commentary: **This is the second time a sinister stranger has arrived at the village inn, with Pip as his object. The links to the Pocket family, and his having previously seen Jaggers at Satis House, make it inevitable that Pip will assume that Miss Havisham is his benefactor. Once again there is a money transaction, a recurring motif in the novel, as Pip is given 20 guineas to buy new clothes. His description of Joe here mixes the feelings of the young Pip with the reflections of the older Pip looking back to this crucial time when he had to part from his family and friends.**

Task 2

Draw a web showing the connections between the characters with Miss Havisham at the centre.

Chapter 19

Pip and Biddy fall out because Pip is patronising to Joe and unfair to her. Pip goes to Mr Trabb's the tailor for a new suit. Pumblechook tries to claim that he was instrumental in bringing about Pip's good fortune. Pip takes leave of Miss Havisham and sets out from the forge for London.

Commentary: **Pip wastes no time in adopting superior airs. Although Trabb's boy mocks Pip for his pretension, Trabb and Pumblechook's obsequious and fawning reactions to 'the stupendous power of money' are, in contrast, more typical. The overindulgence in food and wine at Pumblechook's is a** foretaste of Pip's life of excess in London. Miss Havisham enjoys taunting Sarah Pocket with the implication that she is Pip's 'fairy godmother', so once again Pip's error is confirmed. Pip's first phase ends with his lonely coach journey to 'the world lay spread before me'.

❮ Top *ten quotation*

Volume II

Chapter 20

Pip has a chance to examine Jaggers's gloomy office in Little Britain, the meat market Smithfield, and Newgate Prison. He realises, through watching Jaggers's dealings with his clients, how powerful the lawyer is. Pip is sent to live with Herbert Pocket at Barnard's Inn, accompanied by Jaggers's clerk, Wemmick.

Commentary: **Pip's first view of London is of a black, dismal and degrading place, tainted by death and criminality. Hanging is mentioned again. The death masks in Jaggers's office are an example of a pairing and another case of humans turned into objects. Jaggers is a kind of god in this environment, with the power of life and death over his clients. We learn later that he was also able to bring back Magwitch from oblivion and give life to baby Estella. However, none of his actions has a healthy outcome, and nor will his guardianship of Pip, as Jaggers warns him.**

Chapter 21

Wemmick takes Pip to the decaying Barnard's Inn. Herbert turns out to be the 'pale young gentleman' already known to Pip.

Commentary: **Wemmick is a reified comic wooden caricature with a mouth like a postbox, but also one associated with death because of his collection of mourning jewellery or 'portable property'. A graveyard is conjured again by Barnard's Inn, which is also reminiscent of Satis House, an effect reinforced by the ghostly reappearance of Herbert. Pip is nearly guillotined by a window, another echo of capital punishment.**

Task 3

Study the passage describing Barnard's Inn and analyse the ways in which Dickens uses language to make it seem such a depressing place.

Chapter 22

Herbert names Pip 'Handel' and starts to teach him table manners. He tells Pip the story of what happened to Miss Havisham 25 years before and how his father, her cousin Matthew Pocket, was banished for warning her about her suitor. Pip is taken to the Pocket family home and is startled by its chaos.

Commentary: **Pip receives a new identity as a gentleman, but although Handel was an illustrious composer, the connection is with a piece of music about a blacksmith. The question is raised of how a gentleman is to be defined: wealth (Pip has more money than Herbert); etiquette (Herbert has better manners than Pip); birth (Miss Havisham's suitor was technically a gentleman but did not behave like one); instinct (Matthew Pocket is professional and intelligent, but his home is unruly). The meal in this chapter is presented as slapstick comedy. The juxtaposition of the story of Miss Havisham with Herbert's avowal that he will never refer to Pip's benefactor once again reinforces the idea that they are one and the same. The six tumbling Pockets with the comically named nursemaid Flopson and their hopeless 'born to be a duchess' mother is reminiscent of a scene from *Alice in Wonderland*.**

Taking it
Further
. . . .

Alice's Adventures in Wonderland (1865) and *Through the Looking Glass* (1871) have many similarities with *Great Expectations*, in particular the comic surrealism, the references to food and drink, the illogical behaviour of adults, the use of doubles and contrasting pairs of characters, and the bewilderment of the child hero.
. . . .

Chapter 23

The pretensions of Mrs Pocket are exposed. We meet Pip's fellow lodgers and tutees, Drummle and Startop, at the Pocket house.

Commentary: **Mrs Pocket's social pretensions and inadequacies, and those of the 'toady neighbour' Mrs Coiler, reflect those of Pip. This is one more dysfunctional family to add to those of Pip and Estella. Comedy and tragedy both arise from inadequate parenting, unsatisfactory childhoods and family life. We can tell immediately, just from their names, that Drummle will be an unpleasant and domineering character and Startop a benign but ineffectual one, as is Matthew Pocket who is caricatured by his hair-raising performance. Nutcrackers appear as yet another comic but potentially lethal metallic object.**

Chapter 24

Pip visits Jaggers to request money to provide furniture for his shared rooms with Herbert. Wemmick gives further information about the intimidating character of his employer. He invites Pip to visit him at his home in Walworth.

Commentary: **The struggle for survival in London is brought out by the different methods of Jaggers and his clerk, bullying domination and the adoption of a split personality respectively. It is no surprise that the two casts in the office are of hanged villains, one guilty of murder and one of fraud, the two crimes which recur in the novel on different fictional levels.**

Chapter 25

Pip visits Wemmick's 'castle' and his elderly deaf father, the Aged P, thereby seeing a very different side to the legal clerk.

Commentary: **Pip is consistently generous to Herbert and this redeems him somewhat from his faults towards Joe and Biddy. Drummle is a higher-class version of Orlick, a shadowy creeping figure. The double life of Wemmick is a realisation of the theme and imagery of duality running through the novel. Things works in pairs — such as the firing of guns, paralleled here by Wemmick's Stinger. Food is on the agenda at Walworth that, as a place and way of life, is presented as idyllic with pastoral and fairytale characteristics.**

Chapter 26

Pip, Drummle and Startop dine at Jaggers's house in Soho. The strength of his housekeeper, Molly, is displayed to them. Drummle, nicknamed the Spider, is encouraged to be arrogant and ruins the evening.

Commentary: **The setting of this chapter contrasts strongly with the pleasant ambience and gentle company at Wemmick's house in the previous chapter. Jaggers identifies with the bullying, dark-hearted Drummle. Jaggers's compulsive hand-washing is suggestive of hidden guilt, as with Lady Macbeth. A Shakespeare tragedy and witches are alluded to again.**

*Pause for **Thought***

Look closely at the description of Jaggers's house and consider what it reveals about its tenant. Compare your ideas with those of other students if possible.

Chapter 27

Biddy writes to Pip to say that Joe will visit him. The meeting is very awkward because Joe is ill at ease and Pip is condescending to him. Pip learns that Wopsle has come to London to become an actor, and that Estella has returned to Satis House and wishes to see him.

Commentary: **Pip's servant's behaviour and his own treatment of Joe testify to Pip's snobbishness. The reader is invited to feel the pathos of Joe's situation, but also to find his inability to control his animated hat amusing. Being out of place in London is, however, a testament to Joe's integrity and goodness.**

Chapter 28

Pause for Thought

Do you consider that Pip's behaviour towards Joe in chapters 27 and 28 is understandable or forgivable?

Pip justifies to himself his decision to stay at the Blue Boar and not visit the forge when he goes to see Estella. On the coach are two convicts, one of whom Pip recognises as the stranger with the file who refers to the two pound notes. Pip reads a local newspaper item hailing Pumblechook as the founder of his fortunes.

Commentary: **It is ironic that the apparent happy summons to the side of Estella is accompanied by Pip's association once more with convicts and the return of 'the terror of childhood'. The number two is dominant in this chapter, right down to details of the time of departure and the 'brace of pistols' carried by the gaoler. Pip is able to put himself in the place of the despised convicts, although condemning them as 'lower animals'.**

Chapter 29

The new gatekeeper at Satis House is Orlick. Estella tells Pip that she has no heart and is cold to him. Nonetheless, Miss Havisham tells Pip that he must love Estella. Jaggers dines and plays cards at the house with Pip, Estella and the envious Sarah Pocket. Pip returns to the Blue Boar and dreams of Estella.

Commentary: **The reality of the house, Orlick, Jaggers and Estella's warning undermine the fiction Pip is weaving of being a romantic hero who can rescue the princess. Miss Havisham speaks in triple structures, like a witch casting a spell. It is ironic that Pip cannot bear to have Estella tainted by the presence of Jaggers, given what the reader later discovers** about their connection. Pip's betrayal of Joe and his ingratitude towards him are most acute at this point.

Chapter 30

Pip tells Jaggers that Orlick is an unsuitable gatekeeper. He is followed and mocked by Trabb's boy and takes revenge by complaining to his employer. Herbert advises Pip that Estella may not make him happy and reveals his own engagement to Clara. They go to see Mr Wopsle in *Hamlet.*

Commentary: **Although we share reservations about Orlick, it is worrying that he is summarily dismissed by Jaggers simply on Pip's say so. Likewise, the complaint against Trabb's boy, who voices the reader's concern about Pip's treatment of his erstwhile friends, seems to be an abuse of power. The rule of three is applied to the number of times Trabb's boy affronts Pip in the street, like a fairytale sequence of similar but escalating events. It is another example of the interlinking of coincidence and character in the novel that the Satis House gatekeeper should be Orlick.**

Task 4

List other coincidences in the novel and comment on the purpose and effect of the recurrence of characters in Pip's life.

Chapter 31

The play is a farce, causing much amusement of an unintentional kind for the audience.

Commentary: **Like the novel, *Hamlet* is presented as comedy overlaying tragedy, epitomised by a ghost with a cough. There are many such set pieces in Dickens whereby a scene is staged with an internal audience to respond to it, adding another level to the narrative. The novel has in common with *Hamlet* recurring imagery of father figures, darkness and decay, and the blighting of expectations. There is also a graveyard setting to recall the opening chapter of the novel. That Wopsle has an alias, Waldengarver, a lugubrious counterpart to his comic real name, is another instance of the use of doubles in the novel. Much is also made of costume here — as it is throughout the novel for either comic or sinister effect — as another aspect of Dickens's theatrical approach.**

Chapter 32

Pip is informed in a letter from Estella that it is Miss Havisham's wish for him to meet Estella in London. He accompanies Wemmick on a tour of Newgate Prison and observes him in action. Pip experiences guilt about his tainted past.

Commentary: **As always, Estella and criminals are associated, a clue to her background also implying that Pip will never win Estella because of the 'stain' of his own past. The gardening imagery in this chapter offsets the macabre setting and suggests that something good can grow in unpromising soil. The revelation of Estella's identity is foreshadowed by another of the 'nameless shadow' experiences Pip has here.**

Chapter 33

Estella talks about the other Pockets and their jealousy towards herself and Pip, and also warns Pip not to have any hopes with regard to her, even though she has now come to live in Richmond, on Miss Havisham's orders. Pip returns to the chaotic Pocket family residence in Hammersmith.

Commentary: **The comic scene Pip returns to is in strong contrast to the unhappiness of his meeting with Estella. There is a hint of a link between Estella and Jaggers as they pass Newgate. There is a striking triple structure in Estella's description of her childhood, culminating in 'I was', 'I had', 'I did'. Unnecessary details are given of the tea taken in the inn, served by the inevitable comic waiter.**

Chapter 34

Pause for ***Thought***

Do you feel that money is to be disapproved of because of the events of the novel?

Pip's dissipated and extravagant lifestyle is doing harm to himself and Herbert. With Startop and Drummle they join a dining club which encourages bad behaviour. A letter arrives announcing Mrs Joe's death.

Commentary: **Pip is falling into dissolute ways through lack of direction. Herbert, Joe and Biddy are all causes of guilt, and Pip is nostalgic for the simple pleasures of the forge. There is a suggestion that money does nothing to foster happiness, rather the reverse, and that debt is degrading.**

Chapter 35

Pip goes to the forge for his sister's funeral. Biddy tells him about Mrs Joe's death, her plan to start a school and the attentions of Orlick.

Commentary: **It was a convention, actual and literary, for the dying to repent and ask in their final words for forgiveness from those they had wronged, as Mrs Joe does in relation to her treatment of Joe and Pip. The funeral is treated comically as another theatrical set piece. Pip is taken back to the graveyard where it all started. Once more the mists surround Pip when he leaves, suggesting his blindness to the truth, and the reader compares this setting out with the previous one at the end of Chapter 19, knowing that his expectations are not any nearer to being realised and that he is no happier.**

Task 5

Give an account of Pip's return from Biddy's point of view.

Chapter 36

Having reached the age of 21, Pip has an interview with Jaggers, who interrogates him disapprovingly about his debts and says he must live on a fixed amount until his benefactor is revealed. Pip asks Wemmick for advice about helping Herbert financially.

Commentary: **Pip is reminded of Magwitch by the way Jaggers treats him, which is a clue for the reader that the two are connected. Herbert feels 'dejected and guilty', as if by association with Pip as much as with Jaggers.**

Chapter 37

Pip engages in comic conversation with the Aged P at Walworth during Sunday tea and is introduced to Wemmick's intended, Miss Skiffins. It is secretly arranged that Herbert will be employed by a shipping merchant in return for money provided by Pip. Pip has performed a rare altruistic act for Herbert.

Miss Skiffins's 'wooden appearance' makes her another of those Dickens characters who is presented more as an object than a living being, for comic purposes. The meal is used as an opportunity for comic description.

Task 6

List the meals described in the novel and comment on their similarities and differences.

Chapter 38

Pip haunts Estella's lodgings in Richmond. Estella and Miss Havisham quarrel when Pip and Estella visit her at Satis House, where they spend the night. Pip is tortured by Estella's encouragement of Drummle and the latter's provocative toast to her at The Finches Club.

Commentary: **It is ironically fitting that Miss Havisham is now the victim of her own creation, the heartless Estella. Pip is nearing his lowest point and the collapse of his expectations. The 'I saw in this…' repeated construction within a paragraph in this chapter is an example of parallel sentence structuring typical of Dickens when creating drama or evoking pathos, and a reminder of Pip's life in the dark and blindness as a lover and as a gentleman of fortune. His nightmarish visions of Miss Havisham with a candle suggest the guilty and anguished nocturnal rambling of Lady Macbeth. The story of the Sultan as an extended metaphor is an example of how Dickens interweaves other narratives and allusions to literary works into this novel, to enrich the narrative texture and to convey the imagination of Pip. This is a particularly strong example of a cliffhanger chapter ending.**

Chapter 39

Two years have passed and Pip has moved to quarters in the Temple. A stranger arrives one stormy night when Herbert is away, who turns out to be Magwitch. Pip gives him two pounds to try to get rid of him and then learns that the convict is his benefactor, now returned from a period in Australia following transportation, where he made a fortune in sheep-farming. Pip is disgusted but reluctantly shelters him, as he will be put to death if caught.

Commentary: **The storm is used as pathetic fallacy to create an atmosphere of impending horror. There are echoes of the ghost scene from *Hamlet* in the bad weather, the lack of light, the reference to the striking of the hour and the 'voice from the darkness beneath'. The reader sees Magwitch as Pip sees him and can understand his revulsion while also pitying the convict. The two one-pound notes — and their burning — are symbolic of a futile attempt to return things to how they were before Pip ever met the convict. Magwitch's motives are complex; they include a desire for revenge on society as well as gratitude (to**

The reader sees Magwitch as Pip sees him

Pip and to fate for allowing him 'liberty and money'), and the desire to be the proud owner of a gentleman to call 'my boy'. Pip has finally found his 'second father', and it is appropriately the one who appeared from behind his first father's tombstone.

Pip's revulsion is impressed on the reader by the triple structure of 'The abhorrence...the dread...the repugnance' and his despair in the repetition of 'I could never, never, never, undo what I had done', echoing the anguish of Macbeth, also alluded to in the fear of the knocking at the door. Magwitch theatrically performs a charade of himself on the marshes to aid Pip's recognition of him. Pip feels, as a mirroring of Chapter 1, that his world has 'begun to surge and turn'. There are multiple ironies in Magwitch's offer to buy Estella for Pip: that she is his own daughter, that she cannot be bought for Pip but has been bought by Drummle, that Magwitch naively believes money can buy anything in Victorian society — it cannot buy respectability.

〈 Top *ten quotation*
〈 Top *ten quotation*

It is difficult to predict what will now happen to Pip and his 'dreadful burden', but the imagery at the end of the chapter is full of foreboding: striking clocks, wasted candles, dead fire, increased wind and rain and 'thick black darkness'. This is the equivalent of the end of Act 3 in tragic drama, when all is lost for the main character and those closest to him. Pip's dreams have gone forever with the rending of the veil of ignorance.

This is the end of the second volume of the 1861 edition.

Task **7**

Where does your sympathy lie after reading Chapter 39?

Volume III

Chapter 40

A man is seen hiding on the staircase. Jaggers confirms the identity of Pip's benefactor. Pip is concerned for Magwitch's safety, although still disgusted by his habits. He swears the returned Herbert to secrecy.

Commentary: **The 'lurker on the stairs', the night watchman and idea of spying are characteristics of *Hamlet*. It is doubly ironic that Pip finds disgusting the very 'low' traits in Magwitch, now his 'Uncle Provis', which he himself had as a child and which he would still have if Magwitch's money had not enabled him**

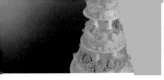

to acquire more gentlemanly manners of dress and eating. The reference to *Frankenstein* by 'the imaginary student' is double-edged and poignant; Magwitch is the monster who wants to be loved by his creator, but he has created the monster of Pip and the two are chained together. Chains are not only another example of an iron image in the novel but also one with connotations of manacled criminals, dangerous dogs and locked gates. They also convey the idea of cause and effect; the chain of linked events that began in Chapter 1 in the churchyard has led directly to this point. In a novel about objects and objectivisation, Provis is now enjoying his 'ownership' of Pip, whose gentlemanly status is displayed by his clothing. Pip's response is to show an ability to think altruistically, which has only previously surfaced in relation to Herbert. Ironically Magwitch may yet do Pip some good and bring out the best in him. Even in this chapter Dickens cannot restrain his use of humorous similes: equating Pip's inability to formulate a plan with the likelihood of him 'forming an elephant', and his housekeeper's niece's head being 'not easily distinguishable from her dusty broom'.

Ironically Magwitch may yet do Pip some good…

Chapter 41

Pip and Herbert plan to take Provis abroad, without his knowledge. They ask him to tell them about his past.

Commentary: **Pip claims that he can detect Herbert's revulsion of Provis. This may be a projection of his own feelings or it may be to alleviate the reader's lack of sympathy towards Pip's own attitude to him. Pip is terrified of adding the murder of Magwitch — by not taking him to safety — to all his other real or imagined causes of guilt. From now on the plot and characters will be pressured by time and timing, as in a tragic drama. The influence of the past on the present and the future will become increasingly apparent and seemingly inevitable.**

Chapter 42

Magwitch tells of a childhood of poverty and crime that led to his association with Compeyson, following the latter's partnership with Miss Havisham's half-brother who helped him to defraud her. Because Compeyson was a gentleman, Magwitch was given a much heavier sentence than him for circulating stolen notes. It was to avenge this injustice that Magwitch fought with and caused the recapture of Compeyson on the marshes, even though this meant his own recapture too.

Commentary: **This chapter is an internal narrative told largely in Magwitch's own words, which provides a different voice as well as information not otherwise available. Dickens's social conscience is prominent here and the blame for the creation of criminals is attributed to the negligence of parents. He also attacks the class system and its prejudices, based on appearance and manner of speech. Doubles are prominent in this chapter: there are two defendants in the dock, the younger and the elder, and the judge treats them as opposites, one 'well brought up' and the other 'ill brought up', as if they are characters in a fairytale. The facts that Compeyson's whereabouts are unknown and that Magwitch had a wife are seeds sown for later. The voices of not only Compeyson but also his wife, two characters we do not otherwise hear speak in the novel, add the fourth level of discourse: author; narrator; character; character quoting another character. The manner of bringing the Satis House story together with that of the convicts on the marshes is dramatic.**

*Pause for **Thought***

How effective is Dickens's structural decision to have the character of Magwitch bring the voices of *other* characters into his own narrative?

Chapter 43

Pip decides he needs to see Miss Havisham and Estella before he leaves with 'Provis'. While staying at the Blue Boar he encounters Drummle and thinks he also sees Orlick.

Commentary: **The sharks are circling around Estella and Magwitch, and the cast of characters of town and country continue to cross each other's paths coincidentally in a manner characteristic of romance. Pip and Drummle compete over the inn fire. The latter's mistreatment of his horse is an indication of how he will treat Estella, and of the means of his death.**

Chapter 44

Pip finds Estella at Satis House. Miss Havisham is not sympathetic to Pip's complaint that she could have been kinder to him and not allowed him to believe she was his benefactor. She does, however, agree to fund Herbert as Pip can no longer do so. Estella distresses Pip by admitting that she is going to be married to Drummle. Pip makes a passionate

speech of love and forgiveness. On arriving at the gate to his home he finds a message from Wemmick telling him not to go in.

Commentary: **Estella is knitting, which is a recurrence of the sharp metal objects motif and also suggestive of cool indifference (used to very sinister effect in another Dickens novel, *A Tale of Two Cities*). Pip's speech to Estella, using the triple structure 'You have been…', is rhetorical and melodramatic, to arouse pathos in the reader as well as remorse in Miss Havisham. His ability to forgive Estella, and later Miss Havisham, his acceptance of his burden of suffering and his charity towards Herbert are the Christian virtues that are the salvation of Pip on his pilgrim's progress. Once again a chapter ends with the drama and suspense of a written message.**

*Pause for **Thought***

Miss Havisham tells Pip: 'You made your own snares. *I* never made them.' How far do you agree that this is true? Is Pip the author of his own misfortunes?

Chapter 45

Pip spends the night in a hotel before meeting Wemmick in Walworth, who tells him that Compeyson is watching his rooms and that Herbert has hidden Magwitch at Clara's house. Pip goes there after dark.

Commentary: **Even now, events continue to be interspersed with comic observations on servants and food. The hotel room is anthropomorphised to make it seem threatening and there is a gory reference to suicide to complete the mood. Indications of the passing of time and the exact hours of events build up the suspense and pressure on Pip. The Walworth pig has been slaughtered and is in the process of being eaten; this is not an auspicious image.**

anthropo-morphism

attributing human qualities to inanimate objects for comic or sinister effect

Chapter 46

Clara lives with her father, who bullies her. Pip has softened towards Magwitch. He and Herbert embark on rowing training on the river in readiness for the escape bid by ship.

Commentary: **Here we have another, and unnecessary, domestic tyrant figure in Bill Barley. His treatment of his daughter is in direct contrast to the solicitousness of Wemmick towards his father, one of the very few examples of a constructive parent/child relationship in the novel. Pip's change of heart towards his quasi-father is another stage in his redemption. He has lost his money, status, future, the love of his life, and is planning to lose**

*Task **8***

List the characters in the novel who we only see but not hear, or vice versa. What is the effect on the reader of this partial representation of them?

his home and country; he can now start to find true values of the heart to replace his previous proud fantasies. The chapter ends with a preview of Provis's fate on the river.

Chapter 47

Pip waits for Wemmick to tell him when to activate the escape plan. He attends a pantomime in which Wopsle is performing. Afterwards, Wopsle tells him that he saw one of the marsh convicts sitting behind him in the audience.

Commentary: **The tension is being built up by the delaying of the escape bid. This chapter contains yet another farcical theatrical episode and one with a double level of watching going on — Compeyson of Pip and Pip of the stage. Wopsle's retelling of the event on the marshes is presented dramatically. He describes Compeyson as being like a 'ghost', a word and concept used for so many characters in this novel full of haunting. Wopsle's declining fortunes parallel Pip's. There is a jarring direct address to the reader in the third paragraph. It is Christmas again — the time of the convicts, of ghosts and of Pip committing crimes.**

> ### Task 9
> Draw a table with two columns — in one column list characters who haunt people or places; and in the other column list characters who are haunted by someone or something.

Chapter 48

Pip dines with Jaggers and Wemmick at Gerrard Street; he learns of Estella's marriage to Drummle and that Miss Havisham wishes to see him. He works out that Molly, a former client of Jaggers on a charge of murder, is Estella's mother.

Commentary: **The characters continue to be linked to each other and Jaggers is now at the centre of the web of connections. Estella's marriage will turn out to be another example of an abusive relationship. It is the 'knitting' action of Molly that gives away her relationship to Estella, a clue as in a detective story. Molly's jealous fight with a fellow tramp over a man, Magwitch, mirrors that of the two convicts on the marshes.**

> ### Task 10
> Draw a diagram that links as many characters as possible to Jaggers, explaining the connections.

Chapter 49

Miss Havisham gives Pip the money for Herbert's partnership in the firm. She asks for and receives his forgiveness for her treatment of him. While Pip is taking a farewell walk in the garden he sees again the vision of

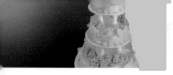

her hanging and returns to the house on an impulse to find she is on fire. He burns his hand while putting out the flames.

Commentary: **In this chapter we see Miss Havisham's need to be forgiven in preparation for her impending death. The imagery of darkness and absence in the second paragraph is plaintively elegiac. Pip's refusal to accept any money for himself and his ability to pity and forgive Miss Havisham, as well as his altruistic request to her to consider the Pockets and Estella, are further stages in his regeneration. Her immolation because of her bridal dress and her laying out on the decaying wedding table, as prophesied, are symbolic punishment for her refusal to let go of the past. The struggle between Pip and Miss Havisham when she is in flames is a deliberate mirroring ('like a prisoner who might escape') of the struggle between the convicts. There are many fights in the novel, some a matter of life and death, which are a motif representing the struggle for the survival of the fittest.**

Context

See the section on Darwin in 'Literary context' for a closer look at the idea of survival in the novel (p. 71 of this guide).

Chapter 50

Herbert nurses Pip's burns and tells him what he has learned from Magwitch, which is that he does not know of his daughter's existence, believing her to have been murdered by his wife.

Commentary: **The fact that Pip was the same age as his lost daughter when Magwitch met him in the graveyard is another explanation for his interest in Pip, as the two children were subconsciously doubled in Magwitch's mind. Magwitch's first name is Abel, which raises the expectation that he will be killed by 'Cain', i.e. Compeyson. It is supremely ironic that Estella is in fact much more tainted by crime than Pip, being the child of two criminals, one a murderess. The chapter ends with the dramatic revelation to Herbert that the missing daughter is Estella.**

Context

Cain and Abel are a biblical pair of brothers from the Book of Genesis, the sons of Adam and Eve. Cain murders Abel out of jealousy. Like Magwitch, Abel is a shepherd.

Chapter 51

Pip goes to Jaggers's office to hand over the instructions about Herbert's money and tell him of Miss Havisham's accident. Jaggers did not know that Magwitch was Estella's father. He tells Pip everything he knows about Molly and her trial.

Commentary: **The whole story has finally been pieced together by Pip, as detective. Jaggers presents his knowledge in the form of a tripartite hypothesis. Jaggers and Wemmick are uncomfortable** when discussing humane issues, the former because he has deleted this side of his nature and the latter because it operates only in Walworth.

Chapter 52

Finally, there is an appropriate vessel bound for Hamburg which Magwitch can escape on and it is arranged that Startop will row because of Pip's damaged hand. Pip receives an anonymous letter telling him to go to the sluice-house on the marshes and he dare not ignore it as it mentions his uncle Provis. He sets off immediately and, after calling at Satis House to check on the state of Miss Havisham, he keeps his evening appointment.

Commentary: **In a further example of parallels in the novel, Pip has now become Herbert's secret benefactor. Another use of a letter is made here to create mystery and suspense. This keeps up the narrative tension which would otherwise have been lost after the explanations of the previous chapter. Pip's return to old haunts is a revisiting of his childhood, and it is not a happy experience. He is regaled in the inn with the fictional story of himself in relation to the 'brazen imposter' Pumblechook. The latter is paired antithetically with Joe: 'The falser he, the truer Joe; the meaner he, the nobler Joe.'**

Pip has now become Herbert's secret benefactor

Chapter 53

Orlick is waiting for Pip at the sluice-house and he ties him up. He wants revenge for being treated worse than Pip at the forge, and for losing his job at Satis House and Biddy. He intends to kill Pip with a hammer and burn his body in the limekiln. He drunkenly confesses that he assaulted Mrs Joe and is working for Compeyson, and that he was the person lurking on the stairs. Herbert and Startop, led by Trabb's boy, arrive just in time to save Pip, having found the letter Pip left in his lodgings. Orlick flees and the three men return to London. Pip suffers an attack of fever.

Commentary: **Pip's rescue is entirely coincidental and just in the nick of time, in the manner of romance plots. Trabb's boy is rewarded with two guineas, reminiscent of the two pound notes which Pip is given earlier. Pip finally feels free of Orlick after this confrontation and admission, and cleansed of guilt as if he has been able to transfer it, though Orlick has tried to blame Pip for everything. His journey to meet his arch-enemy is analogous**

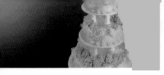

to Christian's journey in *The Pilgrim's Progress* through the Valley of the Shadow of Death.

The change in Pip is symbolised by the movement from darkness to light and brightness during the chapter. The descriptive diction of the first two paragraphs ('dark', 'cloud', 'melancholy', 'dismal', 'insupportable', 'oppressive') is in marked contrast to the cheerful picture of the end ('dawning', 'winking lights', 'warm touch', 'sparkles'). There is a 'veil' being drawn back from London which links with the use of mist elsewhere in the novel. The chapter begins and ends with nine o'clock appointments, one at night and one in the morning.

Task 11

List all the appearances of Orlick in the novel and consider the effect of his recurrence in Pip's life.

Chapter 54

Pip, Herbert and Startop row Magwitch down river, stopping overnight at an inn. The next day, as they are approaching the steamer for Hamburg, a police galley intercepts them. A cloaked figure is revealed to be Compeyson, and he and Magwitch fight in the water. The steamer runs them down, Compeyson drowns and Magwitch is injured. Pip accompanies Magwitch to prison.

Commentary: **Though this is the climactic chapter of the novel, Dickens presents us with another cameo of a comic servant at the inn. The struggle in the river is a duplicate of that between the two convicts in the marsh mud, but this time it is to the death. Abel unmasks Cain by removing his hooded disguise with a theatrical gesture of denouement, but in tragedy the winner must also die. Once again Magwitch is led away in chains.**

Pip has become selfless and, not caring about his own future, has nothing but pity for the 'hunted wounded shackled creature' who had meant to be his benefactor. That Magwitch is fatally wounded by the steamer which was to take him to a new life is ironic, but this gives him a more acceptable end, a non-criminal end, than to be sent to the gallows, the fate which has been hanging over him throughout the novel.

There seems to be no reason for there to be two steamers other than Dickens's love of pairs.

Chapter 55

Herbert goes off to Cairo to start a business and invites Pip to join him later, after the trial. Pip attends the wedding of Wemmick and Miss Skiffins.

Commentary: **The marriage of Wemmick to the 'melodious instrument' and the marriage prospects for Herbert and Clara are an indication that the novel, 'this slight narrative', will have a comedy resolution. The idea of going abroad to make one's fortune, while realistic for young men without expectations in the Victorian period, is also a feature of romance.**

Context

See 'Social and cultural contexts' (p. 64 of this guide) for more on the Victorian period.

Chapter 56

Pip tries in vain to secure a pardon for the dying Magwitch and visits him daily in the prison hospital. Magwitch dies after the trial and before the sentence can be carried out, in the knowledge that his daughter became a lady and that Pip loves her.

Commentary: **One of Magwitch's two children, the real one rather than the adopted one, did become grand and achieve his ambition, although ironically Magwitch played no part in this and did not even know that she was alive. The trial scene is heavy with Christian sentiment, with the use of light imagery, and is symbolic of a Day of Judgement for Pip, and for the reader. Magwitch's passing away is a typically pathetic Dickensian death.**

Magwitch's passing away is a typically pathetic Dickensian death

Chapter 57

Now Pip is home and alone, his creditors move in on him. He falls into a delirium and finds on waking weeks later that Joe has been nursing him. Joe has been taught to write by Biddy and he writes to tell her of Pip's recovery. Her news is that Miss Havisham has died, leaving Matthew Pocket well provided for, following Pip's recommendation. Orlick has been jailed for robbing Pumblechook's shop. Joe and Pip become close for a while, but as Pip gets stronger and is no longer dependent on him, Joe pays Pip's debts and returns home. Pip resolves to return to the forge and marry Biddy.

Commentary: **Pip's serious illness was prefigured by the shorter one in Chapter 53. A near-death experience is often**

used in literature to make a character reconsider their behaviour, situation and priorities, and to bring about their acknowledgement of error and need for repentance. Joe is now, and always was, Pip's 'Ministering Angel' (as Dickens called him in his notes), a 'gentle Christian man', making the moral point that true gentlemen are actually gentle, which Bentley Drummle, for instance, is not. Pip cannot now go backwards, however, so it is inevitable that the distance between himself and Joe will return when he is no longer helpless, and his plans to become a humble blacksmith are unrealistic. His quasi-death and rebirth have been therapeutic, however.

Loose ends are being tied and just deserts are being awarded

The character web continues to link up, with Pumblechook as Orlick's chosen burglary victim. It is fitting punishment for a man who always had too much to say that his mouth should be stuffed full of his own commercial produce. Loose ends are being tied and just deserts are being awarded as the novel comes to an end. The final letter in the novel is written by Joe to Pip, completing the circle of Pip and Joe struggling to learn to write together at the beginning.

Chapter 58

Pip calls in at Satis House, which is up for sale, on his way to the forge. Pumblechook makes a nuisance of himself while Pip is breakfasting at the Blue Boar, accusing Pip of ingratitude to himself. When Pip arrives at the forge he finds Joe and Biddy celebrating their wedding. He sells up, settles his debts and goes to join Herbert abroad. He lives with Herbert and Clara, now married after her father's death, and makes his way up the firm's ladder to prosperity.

Commentary: **This is the third wedding and, therefore, the ending conforms to that of a Shakespeare comedy. The price Pip has to pay for his earlier harshness and snobbishness is to remain single while all around him are finding partners. It is a parallel to Pip's final meeting with Miss Havisham that he should now beg Joe's and Biddy's forgiveness. Pip's leaving of the forge to set off to a new life repeats his previous one at the end of the first book (Chapter 19), though the mood is now resigned rather than optimistic. Pip realises now that he has seen others through the flawed lens of his own prejudices. His good deed towards Herbert has brought benefit to himself, giving Pip a job and a means of making his independent way in the world.**

Chapter 59

Eleven years later Pip returns to the forge to find there is now a little Pip in his place. He takes him to the churchyard and places him on the tombstone. He decides to visit Satis House for old times' sake, knowing that Drummle was killed by a horse. Walking in the garden, which is all that remains, he sees a ghostly figure in the mist, who is Estella.

Commentary: **Exile in literature is always a period for learning and reviewing. There is circularity in Pip's return to the forge and meeting with his young self in the form of little Pip. There is symmetry of feeling in Pip and Estella being brought to Satis House by nostalgia in a supernaturally unlikely coincidence. Estella asks for forgiveness from Pip, completing a trilogy of such redemptory exchanges. Like Pip she has learned and improved through suffering. The fact that once more the 'mists disperse' and there is romantic moonlight suggests that they will not be parted again, although the final phrasing is ambiguous; this is a nebulous reunion and not Dickens's intended ending for the damaged couple, who are in any case both nearly 40 years old and beyond marriage and having children. As in Shakespeare's later romance plays, hope for a better future lies with the next generation, with the little Pip lovingly brought up by the good parenting and teaching of Joe and Biddy.**

Context

See the 'Changed ending' section (p. 50 of this guide) in 'Form, structure and language' for more about the two endings.

Themes

Task 12

List the characters who harm Pip and explain how and why they do so.

The novel is a *Bildungsroman* describing the process of the growing up and maturation of seven-year-old Pip from ignorance and selfishness to knowledge and altruism, through a painful period of two decades during which many of the adults he encounters are hostile or indifferent to his fate and he is his own worst enemy. Many of the novel's major themes are not only typical of Victorian literature but were particular preoccupations of Dickens because of his own childhood experiences and social transitions and insecurities.

Imprisonment

Pip is trapped in a humble home in which he is physically and mentally bullied by his harsh sister and Joe's uncle. He cannot confide in anyone because no one would understand his nature, which is 'morally timid and very sensitive' (Chapter 8). The marshes are 'meshes' from which he cannot extricate himself, however far away he goes; the recurring image of spiders' webs also suggest a sense of being entangled. His apprenticeship to Joe is described as his being 'bound' (Chapter 13).

Task 13

What image or illustration would you choose to put on the cover of a future edition of *Great Expectations* to represent one or more of its themes?

The first person we meet in the novel is an actual prisoner. Estella is trapped in a prison-like Satis House, subjected to an unnatural upbringing with the self-incarcerated Miss Havisham, locked in time. Jaggers represents, literally, the criminal fraternity of Newgate prison, from which Wemmick can only escape through the adoption of an alter ego. That Magwitch is recaptured in the beginning, and finally dies in prison after a foiled bid for liberty, and that Pip and Estella are drawn back to Satis House at the end of the novel, suggest that one cannot ever break free of the consequences of actions and feelings. There is frequent recurring imagery of iron bars, locksmiths, fetters, keys, leg-irons, handcuffs, locked gates, cages, gatekeepers and prisons to reinforce this theme.

Task 14

Find examples of these images and references to imprisonment in the novel.

Money

In Victorian times, money indicated class and was necessary to the status of gentleman, but in the novel we are shown how corrupting it can be. We see the change in the tailor Trabb's attitude to Pip when his fortunes rise, from contempt to unctuousness, and how Orlick's hatred of Pip, and that of the Pocket vultures, is fuelled by his coming into expectations. Pip knows that he can have no hope of winning Estella without money and that money is the reason she is married to the odious but wealthy Bentley Drummle. Pip lives beyond his means when in London and this causes trouble for himself and Herbert; it is partly why he falls ill and has to be saved by the good fellow Joe. The one good thing Pip does with money is to buy Herbert a partnership and with it a secure social position, so that he does not have to be dependent like his father Matthew, forced to take in boys for tutoring and reliant on recommendations from Jaggers.

Miss Havisham employs and controls others through her wealth and can even command the sycophantic Pumblechook to provide a boy for her amusement. However, it was the cause of her downfall in that it made her the target of her step-brother Arthur and his criminal associate Compeyson, and the reason why her family looked forward to her death in the hope of bequests.

The only happy characters are those who do not care about money, who are satisfied with what they have and value kindness instead; that is Joe and Biddy, and Wemmick when in Walworth and not in Little Britain mode. Money changes hands symbolically in the novel in the form of the two pound notes, showing how it links respectable folk with criminals, as does the law, epitomised by Jaggers, who has acquired his money at the cost of his humanity.

> The one good thing Pip does with money is to buy Herbert a partnership

Guilt

Pip feels tainted by his association with the convict from their first meeting and this is compounded by his having become a thief on Magwitch's behalf, even though he stole only things from his home. Mrs Joe makes him feel guilty for asking the questions she refuses to answer. From then on there are many references to crime and images of death, gallows and hanging, and everywhere Pip goes and everyone he meets seems involved in violence, murder and duplicity: Jaggers, Wemmick, Molly, Orlick, Mrs Joe, Drummle — even Wopsle/Waldengarver in *Hamlet*. Only Biddy remains completely free of criminal connection.

Added to Pip's conscience is the burden of guilt towards Joe and Biddy for his wilful neglect, for having unintentionally incited Orlick to attack his sister, for having led Herbert into debt, and for being the cause of Magwitch putting himself in fatal danger by returning to England to see him. A symbol of guilt borrowed from *Macbeth* is Jaggers's fanatical washing of his hands and there are other allusions to Shakespeare on tragedy throughout the novel.

Parental figures

Pip spends the novel unconsciously searching for a replacement father and mother for the dead Pirrip and Georgiana. His brother-in-law is too slow-witted, a man-child, and his sister too unapproachable to be satisfactory surrogate parents. Herbert's parents are unsatisfactory to the point of negligence. Miss Havisham is a parody of motherhood and Jaggers an unlikely guardian. Ironically it is a convict who adopts Pip and calls him 'my boy'. Examples of filial love are given only in the comic form of Wemmick towards his father and, finally, Pip towards Magwitch; there is a noticeable shortage of parental affection in the novel and a significant number of characters are orphans.

Great expectations

There are other characters with expectations in addition to Pip and in each case they turn out to be ironic in their outcome, as is implied by the expression itself. Sarah Pocket and the other relatives who await their bequests from Miss Havisham are disappointed. Miss Havisham herself dedicates her blighted life to avenging herself on men, but finds no satisfaction in her destruction of the nature of Estella and the hopes of Pip. Mr Pumblechook does not get the gratitude he anticipates from the elevated Pip. Magwitch does not get the full satisfaction of having created a gentleman. It is those who have no expectations — Herbert and Matthew Pocket, Joe, Biddy and arguably Wemmick — who end the novel happy and with more than they could have hoped for.

Death

Death was a preoccupation of Victorian writers and their readers. The novel begins in a graveyard with the reading of a tombstone. There are many deaths in the novel and a reminder of it in the echoes of *Hamlet* throughout, and in the recurring imagery of hanging beginning in Chapter 1 with the reference to the pirate on the gibbet. Many of the characters are under sentence themselves or awaiting the death of another in the novel.

Jaggers's office is full of *memento mori*; Wemmick is a walking reliquary and his aged parent, deaf and ancient, cannot have long to live. The mausoleum of Satis House, its derelict brewery and empty dovecotes, is symbolic of death in a wider sense. Even comic imagery in the novel alludes to skeletons and forms of capital punishment, such as Pip nearly being guillotined by a window. References to ghosts remind the reader throughout of the fact of death and that the dead did not always stay dead.

Task 15

List all the orphaned or adopted characters in the novel and draw a conclusion about what they have in common.

Task 16

Who are the characters hoping, consciously or unconsciously, that another will die? Who do they want to be rid of and what benefit do they hope to enjoy?

Context

See the section on 'Death and mourning' in 'Social and cultural contexts' (p. 68 of this guide).

Childhood and imagination

For a post-Romantic like Dickens, childhood and imagination were synonymous. At the end of the first chapter Pip wonders what the cows are thinking and imagines that the convict is the dead pirate come to life. We soon learn that he is a dreamer and a concocter of fantasies. This is made explicit when he tells a fabricated version of his first visit to Miss Havisham's to the credulous Joe, Mrs Joe and Pumblechook. His fearful imaginings and ability to sympathise are what cause him to obey the convict's instructions, setting off the whole train of events. They also set him apart from his peers and make him sensitive to slights and a butt of mockery from the likes of Trabb's boy and Orlick, who are such down-to-earth figures.

Pip morbidly imagines that Miss Havisham is hanging in the old brewery at Satis House, and his visions are a vehicle for much of the horror imagery in the novel. An overactive imagination is a curse in that it is so often accompanied by undeserved guilt because of involuntary identification with the perpetrator of the transgression, a feeling that all sensitive children have experienced.

Task 17

List the examples of dreams and visions in the novel, and comment on their significance.

Punishment

Children were regularly punished in Victorian times by their parents and their teachers. Punishment in the novel takes the form of physical (Mrs Joe's treatment of Pip, Orlick's attacks), mental (the tortures Pip suffers at the hands of Estella, the deliberate teasing of her relatives by Miss Havisham) and statutory (the inmates of Newgate and the Hulks, and transportation to Australia).

Moral punishment is served on the deserving wicked and in an appropriate form: Mrs Joe loses her voice; Drummle falls off his horse; Miss Havisham catches fire; Compeyson drowns; and Pumblechook is robbed and humiliated. Pip's punishment for his snobbery and his moral reformation is brought about by his having to overcome his repugnance and accept responsibility for Magwitch, his renunciation of money and hopes of acquiring Estella, and his self-inflicted exile of 11 years in the East.

Context

See the section on 'Crime and punishment' in 'Historical context' for more on this topic (p. 62 of this guide).

Gratitude

For Victorians gratitude was an important Christian obligation. Pip is able to show his gratitude to Herbert, and ultimately to his 'Uncle Provis', but his ingratitude to Joe and Biddy on many counts is the great sin that hangs over the novel. Others also claim it and are refused: Pumblechook

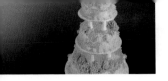

Pause for _Thought_ ❙❙

Do you find it
convincing that
Magwitch would want
to show his gratitude
to a seven-year-old
he met very briefly a
long time ago?

demands gratitude from Pip to which he is not entitled, as he is not actually 'the earliest benefactor and founder of [his] fortunes' (Chapter 52); Mrs Joe does not really deserve any for her having brought Pip up 'by hand' (Chapter 2), though she expects it; Estella understandably refuses to show any to her adoptive mother, Miss Havisham. The chains of gratitude bind many of the novel's characters to Jaggers, for having saved them from the harsh penalties of the law or for having served their needs. The entire plot hinges on Magwitch's need to show his gratitude to the child who briefly and reluctantly helped him one Christmas Day on the marshes.

Revenge

A significant number of the characters in the novel are motivated by the desire for revenge for a past injustice and this links unlikely characters together across class divisions. Magwitch escapes from the Hulks to bring back 'gentleman' Compeyson, on whom he wants revenge for having unjustifiably received a lighter sentence than himself in a fraud trial. Conversely it is Compeyson's desire to avenge himself on Magwitch for his own recapture that drives him to track Magwitch down in London and arrange for his arrest as a returned transported convict.

As a child, Pip feels a need to one day get revenge on Pumblechook for the torments inflicted on him, including the maths problems, and he does so by ignoring him when he comes into his fortune. Orlick wants revenge on Mrs Joe, Joe and Pip for his perceived mistreatment at the forge. Molly kills a fellow vagrant in revenge for stealing her man. The concept of revenge is unchristian and not embraced by Joe or Biddy, although they have been wronged by Pip's having distanced himself from them. Miss Havisham begs for forgiveness from Pip at their last meeting for having tried to avenge herself on the male gender through him. The choice of _Hamlet_ as the play Pip sees in London, in which Wopsle is performing, reinforces the Gothic revenge theme.

Context

See 'Literary context'
(p. 69 of this guide) for
more about the Gothic.

Redemption

Dickens wanted to ensure that his heroes and approved characters could expect to be saved, and that even his less evil villains could show penitence at the last minute. There is forgiveness for Mrs Joe, Miss Havisham and Estella, and Pip's progress to salvation is well charted. Other characters are either redeemed or damned according to their ability and willingness to show charity, sympathy or just basic humanity, and this has nothing to do with their social class, wealth or criminality, but whether they are capable of change and admitting error.

Doubles

The Victorians were fascinated by the concept of doubles, a characteristic of Gothic, which in literature took the form of doppelgängers and split personalities.

Everything in the novel has a pair or parallel, an opposite or mirror image. Hypocrisy is a form of doubling (epitomised by Pumblechook) and actors (Wopsle/Waldengarver) are by definition creators of alternative personae. Wopsle is not the only character with two names or two identities: Wemmick has two personalities, one for work and one for home; Magwitch becomes Provis; Herbert nicknames Pip as Handel.

Dickens also weaves doubles into the plot and imagery: there are two meetings at the Jolly Bargemen; two heads on the mantelpiece in Jaggers's office; two pound notes; two steamers; two convicts; two fevers for Pip; Magwitch receives a sentence of 14 years, twice that of Compeyson. A simultaneous double viewpoint enables comedy to be made from tragic material, which is the effect of giving the ghost a cough in *Hamlet* and the description of the pall-bearers at Mrs Joe's funeral.

doppelgänger

a double or look-alike of a person, regarded as a sinister omen

Task **18**

Find more examples of repeated events or paired objects, or characters operating as similar or opposite pairs.

Characters

Philip Pirrip

Cartoon-like with its alliteration and assonance, and almost a double palindrome, Pip's full name and self-imposed nickname sound both quasi-comic and pathetically vulnerable. Pip is like a pet's name and it foreshadows his adopted role as the faithful follower of inappropriate masters and mistresses whose bidding he unquestioningly performs: Mr Pumblechook's arithmetic questions; Miss Havisham's and Estella's demands to be entertained and admired respectively; Jaggers's prohibition on discovering the identity of his benefactor; Herbert's instruction on etiquette. However, just as Pip named himself he goes on to make himself, allowing — with arguably forgivable intentions — the greed and corruption of Victorian society to be enscribed and writ large on his blank page, proving that social mobility can be at the cost of personal integrity. We can interpret his name as being a seed that will grow and flourish, or not, according to the soil it is planted in and the nurturing it is given, although Miss Havisham tells him that he is responsible for what he has believed and become: 'You made your own snares. *I* never made them.' (Chapter 44). His failing is that he is a child 'whom nature and circumstances made so romantic' (Chapter 30), and that he is a contradictory combination of traits, summed up by Herbert as being: 'a good fellow, with impetuosity and hesitation, boldness and diffidence, action and dreaming, curiously mixed in him' (ibid.).

However, Pip is cruelly misled and exploited by many people who ruined his childhood and ensured that he would lose his way as an adult. Everyone wants to impose on Pip — even Herbert wants to fight with him when they first meet at Satis House and Trabb's boy mocks him mercilessly and publicly. Like many such upwardly mobile characters in fiction, he belongs nowhere. He finally overcomes his aversion to the working class, learns judgement of character and earns himself a genuine fortune during his decade of hard work abroad. There is a new young Pip at the end of the novel to signify Pip's regeneration.

Miss Havisham

She does not have a first name (when Joe refers to her as 'Miss A' this is a comic dropping of the 'H') and is a more distant and inhuman figure as a result. Fearful to Pip, like a witch, she is a man-hater (her half-

---

Task 19

Construct the speech Pip would make in court in order to defend himself against the charge of being a snob, i.e. 'an inferior known for his airs of superiority'.

---

brother, whose surname is Arthur, and his accomplice, Compeyson, cheated her of her dowry and marriage), who withdrew from the world so embittered at being jilted that she adopted and raised a girl child to wreak revenge on the male sex. She lives in an ironically named type of castle with iron gates and a key (Satis House). All her clocks were stopped at twenty to nine, making her seem like a fairytale captive. She represents the unnatural, non-feminine female so abhorred by the Victorians and is a totally unsuitable parent. Her money comes from brewing, illustrating the Victorian

TopFoto

Sian Phillips as Miss Havisham in an RSC production, 2005

belief that self-improvement can be acquired through commerce. She gives an aura of suspense and mystery to the plot, is symbolic of the destructive ravages of time and demonstrates the damage done by hate. The ability to forgive was an important Christian virtue for Victorians, hence her being fatally punished by fire, symbolic of a descent into hell and the traditional form of death for witches. She also represents the corrupting influence of class, power and money, in the way that, for example, her relatives wait for handouts in a cynical exploitation of family connection. Her support of Herbert and bequest to Matthew, the only honest relatives, redeem her memory somewhat. Satis House is pulled down and something more wholesome will be built on the land.

Abel Magwitch

He is 45 in Chapter 1 when he meets the seven-year-old Pip. He symbolically rises from Pip's father's gravestone. His first name, that of a biblical sheep-herder who is murdered, suggests that he, like Pip, is a victim. His surname, a combination of the words 'magus' and 'witch', connotes sinister conjuring and he threatens to produce someone who will kill and eat Pip. He is both Pip's keeper and his nemesis, a good shepherd (to become literally a sheep farmer in New South Wales) who watches over Pip. He conjures up a new gentlemanly Pip, but one who must keep his childhood nickname and never assume the adult form of Philip, because to his benefactor he represents the innocence, pity and charity of childhood, though not a childhood Magwitch himself enjoyed as an orphaned juvenile delinquent. As a 'hunted wounded

Taking it Further ▶

Read Carol Ann Duffy's dramatic monologue 'Havisham', in which the poet creates a voice for Dickens's character, and consider how this modern feminist reworking of *Great Expectations* may shed light upon Duffy's source text. You may also enjoy reading Duffy's 'Mrs Scrooge', which reworks Dickens's *A Christmas Carol.*

Task 20

Using Carol Ann Duffy's 'Havisham' as a template, write a dramatic monologue called 'Estella', which aims to capture aspects of Dickens's original presentation of her character while also providing a more modern interpretation.

Context

See 'Historical context' (p. 62 of this guide) for more about the Victorian period.

Context

See 'Literary context'
(p. 72 of this guide)
for more about
Frankenstein.

shackled creature' (Chapter 54) he is an outcast from society, serving as an example of the severity and injustice of the class-prejudiced Victorian legal system. His alias 'Provis' suggests he has to be tried and tested, proved, or to put himself in the hands of Providence. He is also a kind of Frankenstein's monster, a loner created by imagination and fire who returns to his creator to claim recognition and kinship.

Joseph Gargery

Joe is one of Dickens's divine idiots, a holy fool who neither neglects nor exploits his fellow men. The illiterate blacksmith, 'plain contented Joe', an unassuming salt-of-the-earth villager with brawn but not brain, represents the importance of hearth and home for sentimental Victorians. He is a child-adult who provides much amusement, but he is also Pip's truest friend and protector, using 'his combination of strength with gentleness' (Chapter 18). Dickens told his friend John Forster 'I have put a child and a good-natured foolish man in relations that seem to me very funny.'

Joe married Mrs Joe in order to help with the upbringing of the orphaned Pip, being an 'amiable honest-hearted duty-doing man' (Chapter 14). His goodness contrasts with the behaviour of all the adult neglecters and exploiters — those who have designs on or try to impose themselves on Pip or put him down — though ironically he must suffer being looked down on by Pip. He is capable of infinite humility, tolerance, steadfastness and forgiveness, without recrimination, and stands for all the Christian virtues. He has 'a strong hand, a quiet tongue, and a gentle heart' (Chapter 35). He makes his living by honest industry, to be contrasted with, for example, Jaggers, and those who do no work at all. We are meant to see in him the true nobility of those from humble origins and with no pretensions to a higher status. He is the main focus for betrayal and the cause of Pip's guilt in the novel.

Mrs Joe

She has her mother's first name, being Georgiana Maria, but this is not used by anyone; her formal title stresses her lack of family feeling and distance from her younger brother (it seems by at least a generation). Like Miss Havisham she is a totally unsuitable mother figure and in fact plays the role of a wicked stepmother who stifles the natural inquisitiveness of children and is incapable of sympathy. Although her marriage is a childless one, as soon as Joe marries a second time, Biddy produces a child, suggesting that Mrs Joe is barren or does not permit sexual relations, which would be entirely in keeping with her character.

In Victorian terms she has failed in her duty to produce children. The imagery associated with her is that of sharp metal items: pins, needles, graters and knives, symbolising her unyielding nature and propensity to inflict pain. She receives divine retribution in the form of the 'devil' Orlick, who strikes her dumb and bends her to his will. In a neat application of poetic justice her instrument of torture against others, the euphemistic 'Tickler', is substituted by a convict's leg-iron and is turned against her to inflict an ultimately fatal wound.

Estella

Her name means 'star', an image linked to her as she traverses the dark passages of Satis House with a candle, a lure for moths intent on self-destruction. She is the star in Pip's firmament, the unattainable other-worldly princess, but she has her roots in the criminal world Pip is so afraid of succumbing to. Though a child victim of adult malice and manipulation herself, this makes her harsh rather than sympathetic towards Pip. She learns through suffering — exchanging an abusive adoptive mother for an abusive husband — and both the original and the changed ending suggest that she has found some heart, presumably because she is Magwitch's daughter. There is a supreme irony in her being the haughty daughter of two murderous criminals and one that asks questions about the basis of class distinction in Victorian society. Her rejection of Miss Havisham causes the latter's dejection and carelessness, which leads to her immolation, and thus Estella fittingly destroys the person who taught her to destroy.

Estella…is the star in Pip's firmament

Pumblechook

Though he is Joe's uncle, his affinity is with the grasping Mrs Joe. A seed merchant obsessed with money and status, he is not as comic as his name implies, since he makes the young Pip's life a misery, and the hypocrisy and pomposity of 'that detested seedsman' (Chapter 13) reflect badly on adults in general. Self-serving to a degree, he cares nothing for Pip's future, while wanting to claim every credit for anything that comes of it. His claiming to be 'the first benefactor and founder of [Pip's] fortunes' (Chapter 52) is ironic in many ways, not least in that Miss Havisham, to whom Pip was introduced by Pumblechook, is not only not Pip's benefactor but his potential nemesis. Pumblechook is a 'windy donkey' (Chapter 58) who knows no verbal restraint and enjoys holding forth to an audience, as he does at both the forge and the Blue Boar in town. He is suitably punished by not only being robbed by Orlick, but also by being gagged with seeds.

Jaggers

Pause for *Thought*

Are you convinced
that Jaggers would
want to save the baby
Estella or that Miss
Havisham would ask
Pip for forgiveness?

His name is threatening, as 'jagged' connotes weapons and wounds. Like Orlick, he is large, associated with the colour black, is as sadistic in his way and equally enjoys the exercise of power. He is barely on the right side of the law, given his dubious practices in intimidating juries into awarding innocent verdicts to the guilty. He spends his time with the capital's low life and enjoys the company of unpleasant people such as Drummle because of their entertainment value and their affirmation of his cynicism. As well as being representative, literally, of crime and punishment, he plays the role of the go-between lawyer of Pip, Miss Havisham and Abel Magwitch, thus reinforcing Pip's illusion as to the identify of his benefactor. He is a key player in the plot, responsible for having given baby Estella to Miss Havisham and retained her mother Molly as his housekeeper. His office in the symbolically named Little Britain is a shrine to the macabre, to the money to be made from contact with crime, prison and death, and to the corrupting influence of London.

Herbert Pocket

Herbert
represents
amiable
benevolence

With his comic name Herbert represents amiable benevolence and is a foil to the morally mired Pip. He does not suffer from either a guilt complex or an overactive imagination although, like Pip, he sees events through a distorting lens — in his case one of wishful thinking — since he believes that he won the fight at Satis House. His 'natural incapacity to do anything secret and mean' (Chapter 22) provides a contrast to and worthy example for Pip. He is not a practical business man — his catchphrase is that he is 'looking about me' — which gives Pip the opportunity to perform a redeeming charitable act in arranging secretly for Miss Havisham to buy him a partnership, ironically making her Herbert's benefactor though she is not Pip's. Herbert provides an objective view where needed, of Estella and Provis for instance, so that the reader can gauge the extent of Pip's infatuation or the acceptability of his disgust. His father is professional and he has manners, therefore he enjoys the social and financial status to which Pip aspires and which he finally attains. He finds an uncomplicated wife in Clara Barley, but this Pip does not attain.

Biddy

With her homely and passive name, suggesting she is biddable, Biddy is the ideal kind, loyal and dependable woman, the staunch supporter who will always be there when needed. Like Pip and Estella she was adopted (by the Wopsles) and is an orphan. Her grandmother Wopsle runs the village school and Biddy is associated with education and nurturing; she is Pip's first real teacher, and later Joe's. She is quietly perceptive — for instance in interpreting the 'T' drawn by Mrs Joe as a hammer and thus an allusion to Orlick as her attacker — and she is allowed an occasional corrective opinion on other characters, notably Estella. Most of all she is able to appreciate Joe's qualities. Pip's refusal to take her advice, his feelings of superiority towards her and his failure to notice that she is romantically inclined towards him all reflect badly on him. She has no desire to leave home and is able to provide a child for the forge, thus personifying the domestic and maternal 'angel in the house' of Victorian mythology.

Context

See 'Historical context' (p. 62 of this guide) for more about the Victorian period.

Dolge Orlick

The unattractively named forge worker, gatekeeper and spy is associated with fire, violence and darkness. There is something amorphous and uncivilised about his name, as if he has arisen from primeval mud, and Pip makes it clear that he believes he has made up his first name as 'an affront' to decent people (Chapter 15). He is referred to and plays the role of a shadow, lurking and following, and he gets everywhere in the novel, in both town and country. Jealous of Biddy's affection for Pip, his attack on Mrs Joe is not only revenge on her for being his scourge, but also on Pip for being his rival. He fights the battle of the working class against the gentry throughout — targeting the merchant Pumblechook for his robbery — and disapproves of Pip's expectations and social mobility. He ends up behind bars, associated to the end with the iron of the smithy, padlocks and fetters.

Task 21

Analyse Dickens's presentation of three servants who appear in the novel and consider their purpose and effect.

Character types

Minor characters

There are characters so minor in this novel that we only see but not hear them, or vice versa, or who are only referred to by name, such as Bill Barley, Miss Skiffins, Molly. They are left as shadowy, mysterious, inhuman or threatening in some way. They add to the huge cast of comic and sinister human types who surround Pip, as if conjured by his imagination, and who leave an impression on him, as well as on the reader. The very minor characters in the novel are mostly comic and have ridiculous and therefore memorable names that are often 'aptonyms' — in other words, the names suggest aspects of a character being mocked by Dickens.

*Pause for **Thought***

What do the following names suggest about their owners: Miss Skiffins, Trabb, Wopsle, Startop, Bill Barley?

There are cameo appearances by servants wherever there is an inn or shop scene in the novel; these provide highlights of comedy, as well as functioning as a serious commentary on or parody of the passions and attitudes of major characters. Servants represent a class, as in Shakespeare, and their ability to accurately perceive and puncture the swaggering and complacency of their masters is an important social element of the novel and a reflection of the sympathies of Dickens with the underdog.

Pause for *Thought*

What is the purpose in the novel of Matthew Pocket, Belinda Pocket, Sarah Pocket, Wemmick's father, Molly?

Another group of less minor characters provide opportunity for humour but they are also used to make a moral point and illustrate a theme, often by providing an example of how something should not be done or of the consequences of social or domestic failure. Even minor characters are sketched with considerable detail so that their appearance is made very clear to the reader, distinguishing them from other characters in this and Dickens's other novels. In addition they are given direct speech so that their idiolect can be demonstrated.

Task **22**

Consider the physical descriptions, mannerisms and speech habits of Wemmick and Bentley Drummle. How has detail been used to convey character in each case?

Dickens is famous for his characterisation and ability to create types that become household names. He is also, however, accused of being a caricaturist and a creator of two-dimensional characters, ones which E. M. Forster describes as 'flat' rather than 'round', since they are incapable of change or of surprising us by behaving unexpectedly. Many of Dickens's characters are derived from fairytale and romance and can be categorised as recognisable stereotypes.

Character ages

From Dickens's own notes and references later in the novel we know most of the characters' ages. Pip is seven at the beginning of the novel, is apprenticed, as normal, at the age of 14 and is 18 when he goes to London at the end of Volume I. Pip, Herbert and Estella are all the same age, 23, in the third volume, when Magwitch is 60 and Compeyson in his early fifties; Miss Havisham is about four years older than Compeyson. Biddy is in her mid-twenties by the end, and Joe 20 years her senior, which makes Biddy more or less the same age as Pip. Jaggers is 55 and Wemmick nearly 50.

Task **23**

List the characters under the column headings of 'round' and 'flat' to indicate which evolve and which stay the same.

Pause for *Thought*

Why does the reader get the sense that both Estella and Biddy are older than Pip in Volume I? Why does the reader think of Miss Havisham as more than 56 when she dies, and why do you think Dickens made her older than her fiancé, which was unusual at the time? How old do you think Mrs Joe is at the start of the novel and why do you think so?

Character interrelationships

The novel has links between characters from different backgrounds and many characters play dual roles or show different faces in different contexts, which extends the range of their relationships and how they are perceived by others. (This integration leads to a high degree of coincidence and some lack of credibility, but this is typical of the romance genre.) To emphasise their dual nature and changing circumstances, several characters actually have more than one name.

Task **24**	Task **25**
List the characters who function in two entirely different worlds or modes.	List as many coincidences as you can think of in the novel where characters' paths fortuitously and unexpectedly cross.

Character pairings

Most of the characters in the novel can be coupled with others who are similar or opposites. Pairs are sometimes younger and older versions of each other, or characters who have similar aspirations or experiences. Some possible pairings are initially surprising, but their alliance is caused by their treatment of or by Pip, around whom everything revolves and who is the only consciousness we are given as a viewpoint in the novel. Pip alone can be interpreted as a double character, part Joe and part Orlick.

Task **26**
Draw up two columns, headed 'Similar' and 'Contrasting' and list pairs of characters in each, giving reasons for their similarity or contrast.

*Pause for **Thought***

How far do you feel that Dickens has successfully conveyed Magwitch as both a monster of nightmares and a devoted father figure? What has made it possible for these two roles to be played by one character?

*Pause for **Thought***

What does Pip have in common with Joe, and what with Orlick?

Form, structure and language

This section is designed to offer you information about the three strands of Asssessment Objective 2 (see p. 79). This AO requires you to demonstrate detailed critical understanding in analysing the ways in which form, structure and language shape meanings in literary texts. To a certain extent these three terms should, as indicated elsewhere, be seen as fluid and interactive. Remember, however, that in the analysis of a novel such as *Great Expectations* aspects of form and structure are at least as important as language. You should certainly not focus your study merely on lexical features of the text. Many features of form, structure and language in *Great Expectations* are further explored elsewhere in this book in scene summaries and in exemplar essays.

Form

Task 27

For each of the genres listed, give examples of features of the novel that are characteristic of them.

Mixed genres

Great Expectations contains elements of many different types of fiction: detective; horror; mystery; romance; thriller; *Bildungsroman*; social comedy; confessional; melodrama. You might not be familiar with all these categories, so here are a few definitions:

- *Bildungsroman* a novel about the early years of a character's life that chronicles his or her growth to maturity; other famous examples are Charlotte Brontë's *Jane Eyre* and Dickens's *David Copperfield*
- **social comedy** a text that provides humour by poking fun at the behaviour and culture of a specific social group
- **confessional** a text in which someone admits to their sins and errors as an act of penance, which can resemble the Christian act of religious confession

To the extent that the novel is an account of growing up on the Kent marshes, then moving to London and being ashamed of home, and moving between social classes and feeling secure in neither of them, this is also an autobiographical novel.

Great Expectations is also heavily influenced by the theatre, which Dickens was very interested in.

Fairytale

Above all, *Great Expectations* is a romance, and a range of fairytale figures can be identified in the cast of characters. Many of these are specifically named in the text — for example, Miss Havisham is called the 'Witch of the place' (Chapter 11) and 'the fairy godmother' (Chapter 19). (It is revealing of the extent of Pip's delusion that for him she has changed from one to the other.) That Pip has romantic dreams is confirmed when he says he believes his mission is to 'do all the shining deeds of the young Knight of romance, and marry the Princess' (Chapter 29).

Pause for **Thought**

The writer and critic G. K. Chesterton said that Dickens was 'a mythologist rather than a novelist'. What do you think he meant by this?

❰ Top *ten quotation*

Task **28**

List other characters in the novel who match fairytale stereotypes.

Task **29**

Write the storyline of the novel as a fairytale in one paragraph, beginning 'Once upon a time' and using appropriate features of form, structure and language.

Tragi-comedy

In Dickens's own words, *Great Expectations* is a 'tragi-comic conception'. It has the sense of closure and settlement of a comedy, though the ending does not definitely promise future happiness, even in its changed form. The hopeful note is muted, suffused by winter melancholy, with a recognition that so much time and opportunity have been lost and so much suffering caused through misconceptions and disappointments. And it is, after all, a novel about 'the terror of childhood' (Chapter 28). By the end Pip has no relatives and no prospect of having children. There are characters who led miserable lives and are now dead, in particular Mrs Joe, Miss Havisham and Magwitch.

The past still exerts a hold over Pip and Estella, both drawn back to the demolished house. Pip admits that he did not even enjoy being with Estella on the occasions it was possible: 'I never was happy with her, but always miserable' (Chapter 33). Pip has no happy memories of his life since Estella came into it and had none before that either. Furthermore, the novel can be seen as an indictment of Victorian English society, with its damaging class divisions, corrupt legal system, obsession with money and lack of love, even or especially within families or between couples.

Changed ending

Dickens bowed to the expectations of his public and the advice of fellow novelist Edward Bulwer-Lytton in producing a happier ending than the one he originally wrote. The second is in keeping with the tone and atmosphere of the novel, but the first may be more convincing in the context of the character of Estella. Here is the ending published in the last serial instalment, described by Edmund Wilson as 'perfect in tone and touch':

> It was two years more, before I saw herself. I had heard of her as leading a most unhappy life, and as being separated from her husband who had used her with great cruelty and had become quite renowned as a compound of pride, brutality, and meanness. I had heard of the death of her husband (from an accident consequent on ill-treating a horse), and of her being married again to a Shropshire doctor, who against his interest, had once very manfully interposed, on an occasion when he was in professional attendance on Mr Drummle and had witnessed some outrageous treatment of her. I had heard that the Shropshire doctor was not rich and that they lived on her own personal fortune.
>
> I was in England again — in London, and walking along Piccadilly with little Pip — when a servant came running after me to ask would I step back to a lady in a carriage who wished to speak to me. It was a little pony carriage, which the lady was driving, and the lady and I looked sadly enough on one another.
>
> 'I am greatly changed, I know; but I thought you would like to shake hands with Estella too, Pip. Lift up that child and let me kiss it!' (She supposed the child, I think, to be my child.)
>
> I was very glad afterwards to have had the interview; for, in her face and in her voice, and in her touch, she gave me the assurance that suffering had been stronger than Miss Havisham's teaching, and had given her a heart to understand what my heart used to be.

Three-volume novel

The novel is a series of climaxes, necessitated by its serial publication in weekly instalments between 1860 and 1861 in *All the Year Round*. When

Task 30

Many critics have disagreed about which is the more satisfactory ending. Find as many critics' views on the ending as you can using a library or the internet and analyse which interpretation(s) you find the most convincing and why.

it was collected in book form it was, typically for the period, bound in three volumes, each containing 19 or 20 chapters, which represent the stages in Pip's expectations. They also conform to the three Christian stages of innocence, sin and redemption through suffering. Having erred, Pip must lose everything and adopt humility in order to regain his soul.

Dickens occasionally interpolates what appears to be his authorial voice into the narrative for didactive purpose; examples occur at the beginning of Chapter 14: 'It is a most miserable thing to feel ashamed of home. There may be black ingratitude in the thing, and the punishment may be retributive and well deserved; but, that it is a miserable thing, I can testify' and in Chapter 47: 'Why did you who read this, commit that not dissimilar inconsistency of your own, last year, last month, last week?'

A trademark of the novel's narrative method is the intertwining of comic and serious elements even within the same chapter; for instance in Chapter 4 the Christmas Day dinner at the forge is presented humorously and yet Pip is being bullied by Pumblechook and in terror of his thefts from the pantry being discovered. The world outside of crime and horror (someone threatening to eat his liver) are kept in tension with the parody of a domestic festive meal and the eating of pork and gravy.

In addition, the novel is full of dramatic and emotionally charged exchanges and actions, often performed in front of an audience, which give it a theatrical quality and generate tension and suspense.

Naive narrator

Pip is telling the story as an adult looking back to his childhood and youth, and as he seeks to recapture the viewpoint he held at the time, he must keep information from the reader. It is not only his young age that prevents him from realising the truth about various characters and situations, but also his naive and romantic nature, which has distorted or ignored the feelings of others towards himself. The reader must therefore pick up on the clues and draw their own conclusions. We realise that Biddy loves Pip, although he is unaware of and indifferent to her feelings because of his obsession with Estella; that Orlick is jealous of Pip and likely to become dangerous; that Pip is making a mistake in believing that Miss Havisham is his benefactor (although we may not guess who really is) because she makes it clear to Joe on the occasion of Pip's apprenticeship that she has done all she intends to do for him.

However, it is necessary for us to be able to trust the narrator to a certain extent, otherwise we would not be able to judge any of the characters successfully, and we take Pip's word for character judgements which are based on the evidence of their actions and the self-damning

Task 31

Study the last paragraphs of Volumes I and II and comment on the way in which the volumes end.

Task 32

Think of other chapters that juxtapose the macabre, frightening or sad with comedy.

Task 33

Choose ten theatrical moments from the novel that could be used as stills to promote a film version of the text.

words they use; we do not question, therefore, that Pumblechook is a hypocritical humbug and Drummle a violent cad. Conversely, the deeds and speeches of Herbert make it clear that he is a kind and virtuous young man and that Pip is right to be fond of him.

Where the narrator goes astray in his verdicts is where Estella is concerned — because he is unable to be objective and will not hear a word said against her or Miss Havisham — and where his snobbery gets in the way of his ability to appreciate what Joe and Biddy have done for him. He also prefers and tries to justify the romantic version of any event, but as Joe tells him, 'lies is lies' (Chapter 9). Pip will not take heed of the warning and his attempt to be the prince in a fairytale leads to his life becoming unravelled when the stark truth is revealed.

In order to convey to the reader information that Pip cannot know, other temporary narrators are employed to relate past events. Herbert tells Pip about Miss Havisham's past in Chapter 22, Magwitch tells the story of his own life in Chapter 42, and Jaggers fills in the details of Estella's early years in Chapter 51. Each of these has a very different style of delivery, so that the extra narrators add to the range of voices in the novel as well as providing the facts that complete the gaps in the overall narrative and solve the mystery.

Irony

Task 34

Think of other examples of irony in the novel.

There are many ironies of situation in the novel, the most painful being Pip's reaction to the arrival of Magwitch in Chapter 39, where he tries to give him two one-pound notes to repay his debt. Another is in Chapter 58 when Pip arrives at the forge to propose to Biddy, only to discover she has on that very day become the next Mrs Joe. This latter case relies on the device of timing, whereby if something had happened only a few hours before, all might have been different.

Task 35

List the characters who are satirised in the novel and note down which of their characteristics are being ridiculed.

Satire

Through the mockery of characters' attitudes and utterances, Dickens makes sure that the reader gets the message about what is to be approved of and disapproved of in terms of behaviour towards others. He also exposes the contemptuous practices of particular social institutions, notably the law and education, by satirising individuals who represent them.

Structure

Time

The time span of the novel is about 30 years — with the change of seasons used to mark the passing of time — and it starts and finishes in the month of December.

Other time markers are Pip's birthdays and the trips he makes between Kent and London for various reasons which show changes to circumstances. There are large time jumps during his apprenticeship and when he goes abroad for 11 years.

Place

The settings for events in the novel are divided between Kent and London, representing the opposites of remote rural life and the bustling capital. The Blue Boar in town acts as a staging post between the opposing worlds of the country and the city.

Some characters appear in both the country and the city, but most are confined to one or the other. Movement between the two places is a general structural device as many of the characters, not only Pip, journey from one to the other and the plot depends upon their doing so. It is one of the many dualities in the novel that these two settings of village and capital represent very different human qualities and experiences, so that some of the characters seem out of place in one of them, some start in one and end in the other, and some refuse to go anywhere at all.

Coincidence

A structural feature of the novel is the recurrence of coincidental meetings between Pip and other characters, many of whom are surprisingly out of their usual environment. These unplanned crossings of paths form a web of relationships which adds to the idea of imprisonment and punishment; Pip cannot escape and must face the consequences of his previous behaviour towards others.

Circularity

On finding Little Pip seated in his old chimney corner in the forge, Pip takes him to the churchyard as if to return to the beginning of the narrative and to lay the ghosts to rest. The end is contained in the beginning; Pip becomes what he is because of an action performed as

Task 36

List the settings used in the novel for key events.

Task 37

Make lists of those characters associated with Kent, those with London and those who move between the two. What can be deduced from your lists?

Task 38

Give examples of chance meetings Pip has with other characters in an unexpected context and comment on their effect in the novel.

a seven-year-old child which forged the first link of a chain. The novel begins and ends on a cold December evening.

Shadowing and mirroring

Foreshadowing is used to create tension and warn the reader in advance of the undesirable events that are going to happen, particularly noticeable in the case of Orlick's shady movements and Wopsle's preoccupation with tragedy. Mirroring of events is another structural device that reinforces the theme of doubles and forces comparisons and connections to be made between characters and places, however unlikely — for example, the fight between Pip and 'the pale young gentleman' mirrors that between Joe and the dark creature Orlick. In both cases there is a female spectator who is excited by the battle between the males, imagining the conflict is on her account and therefore making her a romantic heroine.

Task 39

Give examples of duplicated events in the novel.

Triple matrimony

The final section of the novel obeys the rules of comedy, as in Shakespeare and Jane Austen, by bringing together three well-suited couples in marriage: Joe and Biddy, Wemmick and Miss Skiffins (who otherwise need not exist) and Herbert and Clara. Estella's marriage to Drummle cannot ever have been a happy one. That Estella and Pip do not marry, that Jack does not get Jill, is made the more poignant by the pairing of so many other characters.

Meals

Meals occur regularly throughout the novel and whenever characters dine together in various combinations, or Pip dines alone, precise details of the food and setting are given. The mood can be convivial or sombre and is often contrasted ironically with the occasion and expectations, so that celebratory meals seem funereal and funeral meals are comic. Food is used in various ways in Dickens: to reveal character and manners, to show class differences of diet, to create humour of a slapstick nature, to create drama when they are disturbed (as in *Macbeth*) and to create irony when enemies are forced to sit at the same table and share a meal, as Pip and Drummle do.

Task 40

List the mealtime gatherings that take place in the novel and comment on the purpose and effect of each.

Clothing

Descriptions of clothing are used to show job and social status, create bizarre looking characters and situations for comic purposes, and to indicate transitions, as a change of clothes symbolises change of another kind. The most significant is the new suit of clothes Pip has made by Trabb, and mocked by Trabb's boy, to represent his new station as a gentleman. The emphasis on costume and gesture contributes to the theatricality of the novel. Unlike in Shakespeare, where clothing is often a disguise, in Dickens clothing is symptomatic of the character of the wearer.

Symbolism

The symbolism of the novel gives it integrity. The most obvious symbols are places and the elements water, fire and earth. The river connects the two settings of the novel: the Kent marshes and London. The forge is security and the cosiness in the chimney corner ('there was no fire like the forge fire and the kitchen fire at home', Chapter 34), but it is also a place of heat and darkness ('Joe's furnace was flinging a path of fire across the road', Chapter 11), a depiction of hell, the source of manacles and, seemingly, Orlick. At the sluice-house Orlick torments Pip with fire and Pip is burnt during his attempt to save Miss Havisham. Fever is a form of burning up and Pip's fiery illness is a purgatorial episode from which he emerges renewed.

The graveyard is a significant place, not just in being a monument to death but as a stimulus for Pip's imagination, and the convict who will later claim Pip as his son appears to rise symbolically from the tomb of his father. The marshes are a mixture of water and earth, smothered by mist, a flat and miserable landscape reflecting Pip's lonely and limited childhood. It is an environment as unlike the Garden of Eden as the rank wilderness surrounding Satis House and one that suggests that mud and weeds have won a Darwinian struggle for supremacy over hills, trees and anything beautiful in nature. Magwitch is presented as a creature of mud, a frog or an eel, filthy and hideous and as if generated from the primordial slime.

Water and fire are causes of death in the novel and the battle between them is used figuratively: 'Then, the ends of the torches were flung hissing into the water, and went out, as if it were all over with him' (Chapter 5) and Magwitch's death does indeed result from being flung into the water. Estella is explicitly compared to a star ('her light came along the long dark passage like a star', Chapter 8) and to a candle which burns moths. She is also a white yacht in contrast to the prison ship ominously called the Hulks, which is described as the 'wicked Noah's ark' (Chapter 5).

Task 41

Give other examples of the use of items of clothing in the novel.

Task 42

Think of examples of other references to the elements in the novel, including those to weather, and comment on their significance.

❮ Top **ten quotation**

Context

See 'Biographical context' (p. 60 of this guide) for more on Dickens's views on hangings.

Hanging

Hanging was the form of capital punishment used in Britain at the time the novel is set and public hangings were a spectator sport for Londoners, including Dickens. References to hanging in the novel occur so often that they count as a structural device. The first chapter contains a gibbet and Magwitch narrowly escapes being hanged in Newgate at the end of the novel. Pip associates Miss Havisham with hanging because of his hallucination in the old brewery.

Task **43**

Why do you think Dickens uses the hanging motif?

Ghosts

Ghosts enjoyed a heyday in Victorian times and they keep appearing in this novel, starting with the convict seeming to be the pirate's ghost in Chapter 1. They are a key feature of the horror genre and they reinforce the themes of crime, death and retribution, haunting the living and beckoning them towards death, like the ghost of Hamlet's father. Satis House is the perfect setting for ghosts and even the living behave like apparitions — for example, Orlick, Compeyson and Miss Havisham. Magwitch's return is a very unwelcome visitation by the ghost of Christmas past for gentleman Pip in his new surroundings.

Context

See the section on 'Gothic and ghosts' in 'Literary context' (p. 69 of this guide).

Language

Detail

George Orwell ascribed Dickens's comic talent to 'the unnecessary detail' he used. For instance, we do not need the name of Pip's five dead brothers on the first page and they are never again referred to. Food in particular is described in meticulous detail which serves to convey a sense of realism and authenticity, as well as making a social or moral point where the meal reflects on those eating it. It is significant, for instance, that Pip is only allowed to eat the despised parts of animals at the Christmas Day meal and that tar-water is used as a punishment in Mrs Joe's household. It must be remembered, that a writer who has a magazine instalment to fill and a story to stretch out over many months is likely to use detail more assiduously than one writing a single volume work. However, it is often the apparently trivial detail which is most memorable in a Dickens description. Orwell summarised his writing as 'rotten architecture, wonderful gargoyles'.

Moral naming

One of the first aspects of Dickens's use of language the reader notices is his made-up names and especially those for comic or vicious characters, whereby their name reflects an aspect of or sums up their character (an 'aptonym'). Characters can be made to seem ridiculous by being given a monosyllabic or overlong name.

Sentiment

It is generally agreed that Dickens is sentimental — though revelling in emotion was the norm for the period. He is known for manipulating reader response by using emotive language and evoking pathos, especially for the sufferings of children and those who are dying. There are several sentimental episodes in the novel, which rely on religious concepts and imagery, and the rhetorical device of repetition.

Further to the criticism of lack of subtlety, Dickens is accused by his detractors of being melodramatic, meaning overly theatrical, in his use of language. The evidence cited is his use of exclamation, repetition and long paratactic sentence structures, all of which can be seen as artificial. Dickens admitted that when 'in earnest' he tended to use blank verse rhythms, which are a device for heightening emotion and moving towards the poetic. He makes much use of the emotive and rhetorical device of triple structures.

Biblical language, including 'Thou', is an example of the use of archaic language for heightened effect and is particularly associated with the virtuous Joe. The six-day creation in Genesis may be being obliquely alluded to on the two occasions that Pip is told to 'come again after six days' by first Miss Havisham and then Jaggers.

Idiolects

Although the general tone of the narrative voice is melancholic (with interludes of comic delight and wordplay), there is a large number of other voices in the novel to offer a remarkable range of humanity of different ages and classes, and their diverse modes of expression. The ratio of dialogue to narrative is high, which is what makes Dickens's novels so effective when dramatised. The direct speech contains idiosyncrasies of pronunciation, as indicated by unorthodox spelling, that go further than being suggestive simply of local accent or a speech impediment and create an idea of the speaker's character and preoccupations.

Pause for Thought

What do the names Pumblechook, Trabb, Wopsle, Orlick, Hubble and Flopson suggest?

Task 44

What sentimental scenes are there in the novel?

Task 45

Find examples of the stylistic devices noted here and consider their effects, to consolidate your knowledge and understanding of the text.

Task 46

Give examples of the idiolect of three characters and analyse what is distinctive about their style of speech.

Class distinctions

The vocabulary characters use is indicative of their social status and can therefore be used against them. Estella mocks Pip for calling playing card knaves 'Jacks' and Joe rarely gets beyond words of one syllable, and even then is likely to mispronounce them. Illiteracy and foolishness can be indicated by a character putting excessive stress on a syllable — for example, 'as–TON–ishing'; by the misspelling of words they cannot pronounce correctly — for example, 'architectooralooral'; and by malapropism — for example, 'purple lectic fit'.

It has been noted that in Dickens worthy female characters of whatever social class are not given regional accents or dialect, so that Biddy speaks standard English although, illogically, Joe does not. The 'guest' narrators are also largely speakers of standard English in order that they have narrative authority and can be taken seriously. Magwitch's vivid speech in Chapter 42 is, except for some lack of grammatical verb forms, fluent, articulate and largely correct; his language in Chapter 1 has been modified to include long and complex sentences, which cannot be fully accounted for by his years as a sheep farmer in New South Wales.

Catchphrases

A further comic device is the use of instantly recognisable catchphrases by even such minor characters as Mr Hubble, who thinks boys are 'naterally wicious'. Mrs Joe is fond of the phrase 'by hand' and Joe is as inseparable from 'What larks' as Mr Wemmick is from his 'portable property'. These verbal tics serve the same function as characters' physical mannerisms, such as Matthew Pocket's need to lift himself up by his hair in frustration and Wemmick posting things into his mouth for safe keeping. The repetition and brevity of these phrases also reveal the characters' limited intellect and simplistic philosophies of life. Blasphemy and swearing was taboo in publishing at the time, so other ways had to be found to convey a character's lack of respect and low morals, such as the sneering Drummle's 'Oh Lord!'

verbal tics serve the same function as characters' physical mannerisms

Similes

Dickens's greatest gift as a writer is often thought to be his ability to create unusual but apt, and often comic, similes. He said of himself: 'It is my infirmity to fancy or perceive relations in things which are not apparent generally' (quoted in John Carey, *The Violent Effigy*, 1991). This takes the form of perceiving relations between places, animals, things and people in a variety of combinations. Magwitch is first described as a dog to stress his low nature and manner of eating; Joe is comically compared to a bird with 'his mouth open, as if he wanted a worm' (Chapter 13); Jaggers is sinisterly similar to his 'high-backed chair...of deadly black horsehair, with rows of brass nails round it, like a coffin' (Chapter 20). The nicknames that Dickens gives people and things — 'Tickler', 'Stinger', 'Spider', 'Avenger' — are a condensed form of simile.

Reification and anthropomorphism

Reification — the treating of people as things — and, conversely, anthropomorphism or personification — the treating of things as people — have a humorous effect because they are unexpected or incongruous. In Dickens's novels there is an easy transference between animate and inanimate, and it is in the border country between objects and humans that Dickens's imagination is most fully engaged. Our belongings express us and outlive us, so it is only a short step to say that they are us and even that they own us as much as we own them. Cruel characters respect neither their possessions nor their human relations, whereas by contrast Joe is very attached to his hat. Objects associated with a character represent their experience, serving as a kind of shorthand and compressed simile: Wemmick is a postbox, containing secrets safely; Miss Havisham is equated with her clock, both stopped; Mrs Joe is a sharp, metallic figure represented by her needles and pins. She is also attacked with the leg-iron that is symbolic of violent crime generally and is a bodily extension of Magwitch, who is also described 'as if he had works in him like a clock, and was going to strike' (Chapter 3). Time is a rodent that gnaws away at Miss Havisham, just as the mice gnaw at her wedding feast.

Dickens is particularly fond of turning people into substances: Miss Skiffins is unpliable wood, like a musical instrument; Miss Havisham is decaying fabric, like her bridal gown; Orlick is unyielding black iron, without conscience or humanity.

> **Context**
>
> See the section on 'Decoration and decor' in 'Social and cultural contexts' (p. 66 of this guide).

Contexts

This section is designed to offer you an insight into the influence of some significant contexts in which *Great Expectations* was written and has been received. Assessment Objective 4 (see p. 79) requires demonstration of an understanding of the significance of contexts of production and reception. Such contextual material should, however, be used with caution. Reference to contexts is only valuable when it genuinely informs a reading of the text. Contextual material that is clumsily introduced or 'bolted on' to an essay will contribute very little to the argument.

Biographical context

Charles Dickens's life and works

Dickens was a household name even in his lifetime and he became an English institution, securing a permanent place in the canon of English literature. He was a self-made man in the sense that he had little formal education and a radical by disposition because of his sympathy with the little man, the underdog, the individual against the system. Writing in an industrial era and living in London, Dickens is predominantly an urban novelist who points out the consequences of the Industrial Revolution for the workers exploited by it and how this dehumanisation affected the professional class of teachers and lawyers as well.

Dickens is predominantly an urban novelist

Great Expectations was his fourteenth novel and he wrote only one more complete one (*Our Mutual Friend*), leaving *The Mystery of Edwin Drood* unfinished on his death in 1870. In addition to novels he wrote short stories and a number of essays and non-fiction works. The range of his appeal to the public shows in the fact that, though he was a champion of the common man and contrary to his own wishes, he was buried in Poets' Corner in Westminster Abbey on 14 June 1870. The inscription on his tomb says: 'He was a sympathiser to the poor, the suffering, and the oppressed; and by his death, one of England's greatest writers is lost to the world.' His reported last words were 'Be natural my children. For the writer that is natural has fulfilled all the rules of art.'

Charles John Huffam Dickens was born in 1812 to John and Elizabeth, the second of eight children. He married Catherine Hogarth in 1836 and had ten children with her, seven boys and three girls. He sent two of his sons to Australia, believing it to be a land of opportunity. Catherine became exhausted by childbearing and 12 additional miscarriages. The couple separated in 1858, by which time Dickens was tired of his 'pet mouse' and having a discreet affair with the actress Ellen Ternan, details of which only emerged after his death.

Dickens was reputedly cruel to Catherine and had an affair with Georgiana, one of her sisters, who was living with them to help with raising the children. Prolific pregnancy was not unusual then, as contraception was rarely practised, and children were not expected to outlive infancy, so the number of surviving children in a family was usually far fewer than those born. This is supported by Pip and Mrs Joe being the only survivors of the seven Pirrip siblings. Birth and death were thus associated and became almost indistinguishable for Dickens from a very young age. He saw his brother Alfred die at the age of six months and his sister Harriet also did not survive childhood.

As a court reporter Dickens became interested in the law and its anomalies and injustices, and also by association felt tainted by criminality, as Pip feels. At this time public hangings were theatrical spectacles for the entertainment of the masses and Dickens attended one at Newgate in 1849 — he was so appalled by what he saw that he campaigned for reform. He also attended the Houses of Parliament as a reporter and developed contempt for it, believing it made the world a worse not better place, especially for the lower orders.

He had an ambivalent attitude to London, a place of poverty, disease and corruption, but it was familiar to him and he found it a source of inspiration for his characters. He was fascinated by the River Thames, which flowed past his childhood home in Chatham, and which appears in many of his novels, including this one.

Dickens wrote, acted in and directed works for the theatre. He ended his life, quite literally, by touring America to give gruelling and dramatic public readings of his works. He was always short of money and the tours were lucrative. He had a strong work ethic and it is no surprise that Pip finally succeeds in life only when he devotes himself to working hard and gives up the idle and spendthrift ways of a gentleman of leisure.

A timeline of Dickens's life can be found on the Literature Guides website.

He had an ambivalent attitude to London, a place of poverty, disease and corruption

Historical context

Crime and punishment

In the late eighteenth century there were 222 crimes against property or person that carried the death penalty in England and many people, including children, some as young as seven, were hanged or given long prison sentences for trivial offences. Alternative punishments were sought and it was decided to transport many of the most serious offenders overseas, first to North America and then, after American independence, to Australia, where they were to set up a new colony. The first shipload of convicts arrived at Botany Bay in 1788 and over the following 80 years more than 165,000 convicts were transported. It was a serious offence for a transported convict to return to Britain and in 1810 one was hanged for this crime. Convicts awaiting transportation were accommodated in 'hulks', decommissioned navy ships crudely converted for the purpose, anchored in the Medway estuary.

Newgate prison, painted by George Shepherd c. 1810

Guildhall Art Gallery, City of London/The Bridgeman Art Library

Newgate Prison, originally built in the twelfth century, was rebuilt in 1782 around a central courtyard. It became London's principal prison and public executions took place outside its gates from 1783 onwards. Conditions in the 'Common' area for poor prisoners were terrible but the well off could pay for superior accommodation in the 'State' area. Dickens was deeply shocked by conditions at the prison when he visited and wrote 'A Visit to Newgate' to expose them.

Marshalsea Debtors' Prison, in Southwark, was most famous as the place where debtors were sent until they could pay off their debts. Whole families lived there and Dickens's father spent some months in the prison in 1824, although Charles was spared the indignity of living there by being sent to a boarding house.

The Empire

The British Empire was in its heyday in the mid-nineteenth century and many young men, especially younger sons or those in disgrace, sought to make their fortune, as Pip does, by going off in search of wealth in far-flung corners of the Empire. British trading companies had branches all over Asia and the emerging markets in India, Hong Kong and China offered great profits to those who did not die of tropical diseases.

The British Empire had been steadily growing since the sixteenth century and was by 1800 responsible for a substantial proportion of Britain's wealth. There was a further major growth in the second half of the nineteenth century, and when Victoria was proclaimed Empress of India in 1876 it led to an outbreak of patriotic fervour and 'jingoism'.

The transformation of manufacturing in the Industrial Revolution was made possible by the availability of cheap raw materials from the Empire, which also provided huge potential markets. Capitalism thrived in Britain (many historians believe that the Protestant church was more sympathetic to capital formation than the Roman Catholic) and family firms, built up over generations, were the backbone of the economy. The new factories and mills lured thousands of workers away from rural villages and into the new industrial towns, causing huge social problems. The invention and spread of railways during the period made goods cheaper and ushered in the era of mass travel.

Iron, and its more versatile derivative steel, were the predominant materials of the Industrial Revolution. It was essential for all industry and transport — not only railways and ships, but also bridges. However, in the novel these materials are associated negatively with prisons and fetters, coldness and cruelty.

One of the reasons why the nineteenth century was viewed as a golden age was that it was virtually free of war. After the final defeat of Napoleon in 1815, Britain fought no war in Europe until 1914. The Crimean War and colonial conflicts had little impact in Britain; they were too far away and affected too few people. It felt like a century of peace, progress and prosperity.

Iron, and its more versatile derivative steel, were the predominant materials of the Industrial Revolution.

Among the intellectual currents active in nineteenth-century Britain, 'utilitarianism' (developed by Jeremy Bentham), advocating 'the greatest good for the greatest number', was very influential and represented a philosophical and rational approach to social problems. The rival approach, that of the 'philanthropic' movement, was based upon emotion — the wealthy feeling sorry for the plight of the disadvantaged — and was generally rooted in the religious practice of giving to charity.

Queen Victoria

Queen Victoria was the symbol of the nineteenth century. Reigning for 64 years from 1837 to 1901, she has given her name to Dickens's era. 'Victorian' is often now used as a term of disapprobation, but at the time Britain's world power was at its zenith and people spoke with pride of an 'Age of Improvement' in technology, politics and society. Victoria's reign was also characterised by her great love for her husband, Prince Albert, and after his premature death from typhoid fever in 1861, the queen went into mourning for the remainder of her long life. Although Victorian England is often thought to be the high point of the Church of England and the monarchy, there were in fact significant currents of anti-religious feeling and republicanism during the period. Like Queen Victoria, Miss Havisham holds sway over and makes the rules for her environment, which she has poisoned with the gloom and decay of unreconciled grief over decades.

Social and cultural contexts

Dickens was interested in developments in science, as many Victorians were, and scientific reason informs *Great Expectations*, Dickens's novel which immediately followed the publication of Darwin's *On the Origin of Species* in 1859. The opening chapter of the novel refers to the evolutionary theory of the survival of the fittest in that Pip's five dead brothers had given up the struggle. The nature versus nurture debate is pertinent to the characterisation of Pip, who was born and made 'romantic', and is also relevant to the blood relationship of Estella and Magwitch. Though there was a crisis of religious doubt inflicted upon the intelligentsia in the mid-nineteenth century by recent biological discoveries, this has not permeated into village life or Pip's consciousness as the novel is set earlier in the century.

The nature versus nurture debate is pertinent to the characterisation of Pip

Class and gender

In Victorian society class was everything and this was predicated upon money, which gave an importance to wills and benefactions as these could lead to social mobility and the ideal of being a gentleman or lady. Just looking and speaking like a gentleman gave one a huge advantage in a prejudiced society, so that Compeyson received different treatment from Magwitch at the hands of the law. A blacksmith, as a rural manual worker, was very near the bottom of the social hierarchy.

As a result of the Industrial Revolution there was the rise of the commercial classes of the towns and a corresponding decline in the power and wealth of the newly impoverished landed gentry. Miss Havisham's fortune comes from brewing.

The greatest fear for women was to not find a husband and be left a spinster, treated as a financial burden on their family and regarded as not much better than a witch by the local community. A woman in her mid-twenties had little hope of being proposed to, which explains why Miss Havisham gives up on life after being jilted, left standing at the altar, in her late twenties. Heiresses were much sought after but vulnerable to being defrauded by unscrupulous fortune hunters.

Travel

The only form of long distance travel available, before the railway, was the horse-drawn coach. They were slow, uncomfortable and potentially dangerous because of the poor state of many country roads. Frequent stops at coaching inns were necessary to change horses, often with overnight stops. Pip's journeys between Kent and London take five hours, although the distance is less than 30 miles.

Etiquette

Ladies and gentlemen were distinguishable by their deportment and manners, which included table manners, hence the need for Herbert to teach Pip how to eat in a way acceptable for dining in company. Pale hands were the sign of a gentleman, as exemplified by Herbert — and blacksmiths have very dirty ones. It is Estella's mockery ('And what coarse hands he has. And what thick boots!' Chapter 8) that starts Pip off wanting to become a gentleman, setting the world of the forge against the world of being idle in London.

Pale hands were the sign of a gentleman

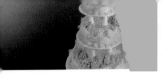

Decoration and decor

Victorian homes, particularly reception rooms, were cluttered with objects and covers on all their surfaces. This was the century of trade and manufacture, of pottery and wrought iron, of clocks and embroidery, and these were all given a place in the parlours of the well-to-do. Many of the ornaments were objects brought back from travels in the Empire, particularly exotic trinkets and amusing knick-knacks from India and China. Fabrics tended to be highly decorative — flowery and stripey and lacy — rather than plain coloured, and cloths were laid over other cloths. Sofas and armchairs wore antimacassars to protect them from men's hair oil. The shaped wooden legs of tables, pianos and even stools were thought to be indecent, so furniture was covered not just with doilies and tablecloths but with covers reaching down to the ground. In addition, pot plants were popular, particularly large ferns and aspidistras reminiscent of warmer climates. This liking for clutter is conveyed in the decors described by Dickens, which are always full of distinctive things.

> This liking for clutter is conveyed in the decors described by Dickens

Education

During the nineteenth century it was common for the education of the children of wealthy families to include a period in Europe. Girls typically went to a 'finishing school' in France or Switzerland, which prepared them to become the wives of rich and socially elite men — hence Estella going to Paris to be 'finished'. Boys went on the 'Grand Tour' to France and Italy to see culture at first hand. Both genders were expected to become competent in French, the international language of diplomacy and high society. Compeyson went to a public boarding school and spoke well as a result and this ensured him advantageous treatment in the hands of the law.

A scene from a dame school in the mid-nineteenth century

Victorian Picture library

Prior to the introduction of compulsory primary education in 1870, the only education available to poor children was provided by village 'dame schools' (as run by Mr Wopsle's great aunt).

Classes were generally large and only very basic instruction in arithmetic, spelling, handwriting and general knowledge was given. Corporal punishment was inflicted routinely in the form of the birch, and since rote learning was the only method of acquiring knowledge, those with a poor memory were constantly being flogged. The illiteracy rate for adults was approximately half for males and two-thirds for females, so it is not surprising that Joe cannot read or write. Pip is right to feel that he will not be able to better himself socially if he does not acquire at least some basic learning.

Apprenticeship

The tradition of apprenticeship — where a boy becomes the apprentice of a master craftsman to learn skills on the job for seven years — was established in the Middle Ages in England. The boy was bonded from the age of 14 and was generally expected to live on site. This would be his trade for life. Apprentices, and indeed all tradesmen, worked six days a week until 1871, with only Sundays and holy days free, so to be granted a half-day off to celebrate something was a major concession.

Religion

It was a religious duty to show concern for and charity to the underclass, to repent on one's deathbed and beg forgiveness from those you had injured, and to turn from the error of one's ways when they were visited upon you in the form of a near-death illness.

The need to appear pious led inevitably to hypocrisy, as embodied in the self-serving sycophant Pumblechook. It encouraged extremes of categorisation into good and evil. From this arose the concept of the Angel in the House, whereby the perfect woman must be maternal, domestic, devoted to her husband and children and the running of the home. Biddy personifies this paragon.

Likewise men had to conform to the ideal of the *pater familias*, the head of the large household of children and servants for whom they had to be a role model of justice and probity. This often led to the hypocrisy of their reading from the Bible one minute and going off to the brothel the next.

Cleanliness being considered next to, or the next best thing to, godliness meant that compulsive washing and cleaning, and the judging of one's neighbours in relation to these practices, was endemic. Both Jaggers and Mrs Joe suffer from a need to wash excessively, as though they have some crime to expiate.

Attendance at church on Sunday at this time is often thought to have been routine and unquestioned, although Victorians were shocked when the 1851 census showed that little more than half the population actually attended church on the Sunday when the census was taken.

Taking it
Further

The full text of Coventry Patmore's poem *The Angel in the House* may be found at www.victorianweb.org/authors/patmore/angel/

Sunday school, Bible classes for children which took place in the church, were an important part of childhood. A side effect of religious belief is sentimentality, with which Dickens is particularly associated. He has been attributed with being the creator of the Victorian Christmas which still lives on to the present day in England.

Death and mourning

The untimely death of her husband Albert in 1861 plunged Queen Victoria into black for the rest of her life. She was only 42 and lived for 39 more years. It also sent the nation into a mode of unrelieved mourning, which took the form of the wearing of black as the norm, an unhealthy interest in all forms of death, the indulgence in memorial brooches or replicas of the dead (which Wemmick collects as 'portable property') and a fascination with murder and all things Gothic and macabre, especially graveyards and dark decaying mansions. This culminated in the creation of the character Sherlock Holmes in 1887.

Death from fever and malnutrition were commonplace and life expectancy for the poor was only 20 years in 1800, although that had risen to 38 by the middle of the century. This meant that most people had lost relatives, especially their mothers in childbirth and their siblings from childhood diseases, even from just a teething fit. Homes were imbued with the atmosphere of the possessions left by the dead. Many thousands of orphans were sent to orphanages where their treatment was, to say the least, unsympathetic, and where they received only limited education.

> most people had lost relatives, especially their mothers in childbirth

Dickens exploited the pathos of dying and dead children in many of his novels, and plunged the nation into a state of grief every time he killed off one of his fictional children, such as Paul Dombey in *Dombey and Son* and Little Nell in *The Old Curiosity Shop*.

Debt

Falling into debt (the verb is revealing) was regarded as a moral failing, as a combination of theft and hypocrisy, and Pip succumbs to it, as Jaggers knew he would. Dickens's father was imprisoned for debt in the Marshalsea in Southwark where whole families had to live if they were no longer able to be supported by the head of the family. Since no income could be generated while the debtor was under lock and key, there was no easy way of getting out of debt and therefore out of prison.

Literary context

Great Expectations was published in 36 weekly instalments in Dickens's magazine *All the Year Round*, in an attempt to reverse falling sales. The first instalment came out in December 1860, hence the setting of the first chapter at Christmas. The serial finished in August 1861. The novel is set earlier in the century, between 1805 and 1825, in the era before the railway and reformation of the penal system, when Dickens himself was growing up. The title puts the emphasis not on the life of its main character but on the delusion that propelled him.

Fellow writers have praised the novel for its mixture of social comedy, farcical humour, violent melodrama and mystery, and it is now one of his most popular and critically acclaimed novels. It is similar in many ways to the 'sensation' novels of Wilkie Collins. The first three-volume edition appeared in 1861 and a single volume edition followed in 1862. In order to make his characters memorable across the time gap between instalments, Dickens gives them immediately recognisable language and appearance traits. *Great Expectations* is tightly plotted in comparison to some of the looser structures in other Dickens novels.

Gothic and ghosts

Gothic architecture and literature enjoyed a revival in the late eighteenth century which lasted through the nineteenth century. This medieval genre of art is associated with the grotesque and the supernatural, and therefore with violence, death and horror. Mary Shelley's *Frankenstein* belongs to this genre and helped to popularise it. The literary settings are macabre, usually ancient buildings, prisons or ruins, and darkness and bad weather add to the eerie atmosphere; Satis House qualifies as a Gothic setting. A common feature of Gothic literature is characters who have doubles or split personalities, the most famous example being R. L. Stevenson's *Dr Jekyll and Mr Hyde*.

The Victorians were fascinated by all things to do with spirits and psychic phenomena, and mediums were in much demand to run seances and put the living in touch with the dead. Inevitably, therefore, a large number of even well educated and prominent people believed in ghosts and even fairies; Dickens and some of his contemporaries — such as Edgar Allan Poe, Bram Stoker and Wilkie Collins — made much use of apparitions and vampires in novels and short stories.

Taking it
Further

William Wilkie Collins (1824–89) wrote intricately plotted novels of sensational intrigue which established the genre of detective fiction. His maxim was 'make 'em cry, make 'em laugh, make 'em wait'. Read *The Woman in White* as a comparison to *Great Expectations*.

The Romantic legacy

Pause for **Thought**

Think of the Pocket
children and the
impression we
are given of their
childhoods and how
they are growing up.

Dickens was something of a pioneer in the field of representing children
in fiction, especially as a male writer, and this was certainly one of the
reasons for his popularity at a time when the concept of the family, and
the dynasties to be created through judicious marriage, was revered. It is
ironic that the picture of family life is not a happy one in this or many of
his other novels, which is perhaps a reflection of his own experience as
child and father. The Gargery, Pocket, Havisham and Barley relationships
and households are dysfunctional and would be cases for social services
nowadays.

As well as a respect for and recognition of the influence of landscape,
Dickens inherited the Romantic legacy of a belief in the innate
innocence of children until they are corrupted by contact with adults.
They are presented as vulnerable, which evokes pathos, but they
also provide a different perspective that shows adults to be not only
threatening but also ridiculous, thereby providing comedy. Orphans are
likely to be more victimised and more sensitive than other children,
and to be more secretive and reliant on their imaginations; they are
representatives of the individual's search for love and fulfilment on
lone and perilous journeys. Pip goes into exile, always a learning and
reviewing experience in literature, and then returns a wiser man, like the
heroes of so many romances and Romantic poems, such as the Ancient
Mariner in Samuel Taylor Coleridge's famous Gothic work. Dickens
admired William Wordsworth and his emphasis on memory, dreams
and fancy, but Dickens was a believer in a dualistic not a pantheistic
universe, one of evil rapacious villains and plaster saintly heroines which
derive from fairytales and owe much to Hans Andersen, for whose tales
Dickens had a special affection.

Victorian readers

Audience demand controlled the content of Victorian fiction and the
disapproval of the readership was a constant threat to authors. Readers
wanted sentiment, just deserts and happy endings; Dickens's literary rival
Bulwer-Lytton persuaded him to alter the ending for the last instalment
of the serial of *Great Expectations* to a 'happier' one. Sexual relations
were taboo, as was any suggestion of blasphemy. The settlement and
integration of the hero into society was the aim of nineteenth century
fiction, to satisfy reader expectation, and this usually took the form of
marriage and/or acquisition of property. It was acceptable for an author
to diagnose, somewhat obliquely, society's ills, though not for them to
dare to suggest social and political reform. Dickens relished his power to

make readers weep and the novels are the expression of the man who wrote them, to the extent of his using authorial interpolation when he had a point to make.

Darwin

The effect of *On the Origin of Species*, published in December 1859, on this novel, started a few months later, is clear. It not only deals with struggling for survival but shows an interest in biological inherited characteristics versus the influence of environment and education, and plays with the idea of the evolutionary theory of heredity. The first page refers to Pip's five dead brothers, 'who gave up trying to get a living, exceedingly early in that universal struggle', suggesting that Pip is somehow better adapted to survive. However, his claiming that he is 'a boy whom nature and circumstances made so romantic' (Chapter 30) and 'My sister's bringing up had made me sensitive' (Chapter 8), makes the reader wonder whether he will. His character is forged in a symbolic and powerful environment, however.

There are many actual physical struggles in the novel that act as symbols of the battle for survival which is part of human existence. The conflict between Compeyson and Magwitch also recalls the Biblical story of Cain (the first and last letters of Compeyson's name are the same) and Abel (Magwitch's first name), the children of Adam and Eve, in which firstborn Cain murders his younger brother Abel. The reader is therefore inclined to expect that the gentler of the two will not survive the malice of the other. Herbert, the 'pale young gentleman' who is physically weaker than Pip, would not have survived in the world of business without help. The most significant fight is arguably that between Pip and Orlick at the sluice-house, where Pip is battling for his life against a demon representing his own dark and guilty side.

Realism

Great Expectations is in the realism tradition in terms of the detailed settings and decors, clothing and food references. The convincing portrayal of the world of the novel depends on the rich proliferation of the physical peculiarities of people and things and places. Victorian novels generally place emphasis on the uniqueness of events and character and are less overtly concerned with types than eighteenth century novels. This fits with the perceived desirability of self-determinism and self-realisation. The novel is directly concerned with the individual rather than the community, and the search for identity makes *Great Expectations* one of the first modern novels. However, fantasy and nostalgia are recognisable elements within the realism and

the search for identity makes *Great Expectations* one of the first modern novels

there is an elegiac note lamenting the ephemerality of childhood and a lost England which led a simpler and more rural life.

Theatre

The Victorian theatre favoured melodrama, portraying the sudden reversals of fortune, the corruption of innocence, the certainty of moral retribution, the horror of the visually grotesque and the pathos of the dying. Dickens's writing draws upon many elements of the theatre of his time, in particular the building up of suspense, the creation of macabre settings and the revelation of secret identity.

Hamlet

Great Expectations has many of the same elements as Shakespeare's tragedy, which is also about dissatisfaction with life, father figures, graveyards, guilt, death, ghosts, criminality, duty, friendship, the cruelty of love and the failure of parents. Like Hamlet, Pip is forced to learn resignation through the experiences of disillusionment and betrayal. The visit to watch *Hamlet* in the novel is treated comically but the parallel between Pip's situation and that of the Prince of Denmark is nonetheless being drawn. The character of Hamlet, who makes jokes about the whereabouts of the body of Polonius, whom he has just murdered, illustrates how tragedy can be treated as comedy if one is only brazen enough to disrespect taboo subjects, a lesson which Dickens applies at every possible opportunity.

> Like Hamlet, Pip is forced to learn resignation through the experiences of disillusionment and betrayal.

Picaresque

The picaresque tradition of a hero on the move who meets a lot of morally dubious characters on the road and becomes embroiled in a fast-paced series of events is apparent in Dickens's work, which makes him a successor of the eighteenth century novelists Henry Fielding and Tobias Smollett, whose work he admired. Pip is often travelling and running into people on the way who, like Alice in *Alice's Adventures in Wonderland*, he finds amusing or illogical, annoying or frightening, stupid or rude. The Pocket family could easily have been created by Lewis Carroll, Dickens's contemporary, with Mrs Pocket and her tumbling infants resembling Carroll's Duchess, and Mrs Joe on the rampage would not have been out of place in a work satirising the treatment of children.

Frankenstein

In addition to echoes of the biblical creation story in Genesis, there are several allusions in the novel to Mary Shelley's *Frankenstein* (published in 1818), her famous work about the scientist and his monster creation, and a direct reference in Chapter 40: 'The imaginary student pursued by the misshapen creature he had impiously made, was not more wretched than I, pursued by the creature who had made me.' Magwitch calls Pip 'my son' and insists he has 'made a gentleman' of him.

Pip accepts that he has been created by Magwitch but it can also be argued that Magwitch was in a sense created by Pip, conjured by Pip's imagination from the mud of the marshes and the tombstones, amid the aura of death and body parts, a kind of resurrection. (There were 'resurrection men' is Dickens's time, who used to dig up recently buried bodies and sell them to medical schools for anatomy practice.) When Magwitch returns he addresses Pip as 'Master', as Frankenstein's monster addresses his creator. There are also other characters in the novel who have been recreated or miscreated.

> *Task **47***
>
> List the characters in the novel who are 'created' in some sense and say by whom or what, and in what way.

Comedy

Orwell says that Dickens's comic gift lies in his use of 'the unnecessary detail', so that the reader is bemused and amused by being told something we do not need to know. Another comic method Dickens employs in *Great Expectations* is the reversal of Romantic expectations and the use of the mock heroic, as illustrated by Pip's account of watching a performance of *Hamlet*, that most poignant of plays.

The technique of giving a character physical proximity but mental distance from a person or event ensures a lack of empathy that is the prerequisite for the character, and the reader, to perceive the other person or situation humorously. His use of caricature is in the satirical mode of Jonathan Swift and Alexander Pope, the difference being that while they are attacking social vices or institutional targets, Dickens is more precisely exposing the failings and absurdities of individuals (for example, Pumblechook who is vilified more for his odious personality than for being a small-town merchant and Wopsle for his lack of self-knowledge rather than his poor acting skills).

However, Mrs Pocket and Mrs Joe represent types, that of the neglectful and the self-righteous parent respectively, so that the comedy lies in the reader's ability to recognise the stereotype as well as laugh at the particular examples of it. These comic figures typically represent those who feel superior to or impose on others. Orwell also said: 'Dickens is able to go on being funny because he is in revolt against authority, and authority is always there to be laughed at.'

> 'Dickens is able to go on being funny because he is in revolt against authority, and authority is always there to be laughed at.'

Flat and round characters

E. M. Forster, writer and critic in the early twentieth century, famously claimed that:

> We may divide characters into flat and round...[Flat characters are] constructed round a single idea or quality: when there is more than one factor in them, we get the beginning of the curve towards the round...The really flat character can be expressed in one sentence...Dickens's people are nearly all flat (Pip and David Copperfield attempt roundness, but so diffidently that they seem more like bubbles than solids). Nearly every one can be summed up in a sentence, and yet there is this wonderful feeling of human depth. Probably the immense vitality of Dickens causes his characters to vibrate a little, so that they borrow his life and appear to lead one of their own...Part of the genius of Dickens is that he does use types and caricatures, people whom we recognize the instant they re-enter, and yet achieves effects that are not mechanical and a vision of humanity that is not shallow.

Pause for **Thought**

Do you think it is true that Pip is more of a 'bubble' than a 'solid'? Can you think of characters in the novel who remain two-dimensional?

Women in the novel

The women fall into the usual stereotypical romance categories of witch or *femme fatale* — like Miss Havisham or Estella — and the homely girl-next-door type represented by Biddy. At the time it was considered a female failure not to have children, interpreted as being an indication of being insufficiently maternal or even feminine; Miss Havisham, Mrs Joe and Estella are condemned to barrenness, although two have been married.

Taking it ▶
Further

Read Tennyson's 'Mariana' (1830) to discover the similarities between her and Miss Havisham's situation of loneliness and death-wish in a decaying, mouse-infested 'castle'.

Although her half-brother and Compeyson are to blame for their criminal intent, there is the suggestion that Miss Havisham's rejection by her betrothed, who is younger than her, is a judgement upon her attractiveness and a rejection of her as a woman. Literature is full of females forced to withdraw from a vilifying and gossiping society to live like nuns, including Mariana in her moated grange in the poem by Dickens's contemporary, Alfred Lord Tennyson.

Critical context

The application of a range of critical theories to the novel would put emphasis on different aspects and interpretations of it.

Marxist

This theory believes that economic factors determine consciousness and character. Dickens was a self-made man and not a particularly happy one. He never got over the shame of being sent to work in a blacking factory at the age of 11, instead of being allowed to continue his education, because of his father's bankruptcy. His family were incarcerated within the walls of the Marshalsea Debtors' Prison and the influence of this environment imbued him with a fascination for and horror of violent crime and debt, and a sense of personal guilt. Pip is also the product of his environment and Magwitch is a personification and a projection of Pip's fears of this environment and of his home life (symbolised by Tickler, the gibbet and chains). The tombstones are a reminder of his abandonment by the rest of his family and the lack of love in his young life.

Pip gains social mobility but at the high price of alienation from his working class roots and the betrayal of his relatives and neighbours. He is never really accepted by the higher class to which he aspires and is forced to leave the country because of this; there is no place for him at home. The Marxist implication of the events of the novel is that prosperity can only be achieved by the creation of an underclass and this class will always fight back, as Orlick demonstrates, because of the social injustice of its exclusion. Marxist critics see Magwitch's creation of a gentleman as a way to fool the class system and get revenge on a society that values people by their money and clothing, and of exposing the fallacy of this categorisation of men according to artificial distinctions.

Marx himself was a contemporary of Dickens, whose works he found too bourgeois in values and sentimental in tone, but which he believed did a useful service in pointing out the evils of child labour and capitalism. However, Dickens is not good at describing people's work (compared to his contemporary Elizabeth Gaskell, for instance) and is vague about what most of his characters — except lawyers — actually do for a living. Certainly he is no revolutionary; as Orwell points out: 'It seems that in every attack Dickens makes upon society he is always pointing to a change of spirit rather than a change of structure. It is

> Pip gains social mobility but at the high price of alienation from his working class roots and the betrayal of his relatives and neighbours.

hopeless to try and pin him down to any definite remedy, still more to any political doctrine.'

Psychoanalytical

The Freudian view of children is that they are corrupted by original sin (which is diametrically opposed to the Romantic view that they exemplify original innocence) and carry a burden of guilt to be expiated as they grow older. Pip and Estella do not have healthy childhoods — they are repressed, not allowed to ask questions or to mix with other children or play, and are turned into drudges and outcasts by adults pursuing their own agendas.

The novel has many references to dreams and dream-like states which psychoanalytical critics point to as revelations of the subconscious. Fire and water are the fundamental elements of Pip's outer and inner landscape and they have affected his psyche, being biblical forces of divine retribution.

> Fire and water are the fundamental elements of Pip's outer and inner landscape and they have affected his psyche

This approach would argue that Magwitch is dreamt up by Pip's imagination on Christmas Eve, a horrible nativity and a creature who must be nourished. Pip was looking for an identity in his scrutiny of the letters of the tombstone. He is also feeling the guilt of the survivor when nearly all his family are dead, and so he conjures the archetypal guilt figure, a convict complete with a leg-iron. Pip then adopts the role of thief himself — stealing from both Joe and Mrs Joe, the file and the 'vittles' — on behalf of the criminal and thus betraying his guardians, compounding his guilt further. To have a criminal benefactor, and the implied social disgrace attendant on it, is Pip's worst nightmare realised, as he is a social climber by temperament (wanting to learn to read and write very early on) and because of his desire for acceptance by Estella.

In psychoanalytical terms the novel is primarily about Pip's search for a father and for his approval (the same quest as in *Hamlet*): Joe and then Jaggers are deemed unsatisfactory, in very different ways, in this role. Finally, after initial rejection, Pip accepts the role of both father and son to Magwitch, Estella's father, and is freed of the need to search further by his adoption of this identity and commitment. An incest taboo, however, now exists against his marrying Estella, a new sister figure.

A further psychoanalytical element of the novel is the compulsive behaviour practised by so many of the characters: Miss Havisham, Wemmick, Mrs Joe and Jaggers all have rituals, obsessions and compulsions.

Feminist

Women in Victorian fiction are presented as biblical stereotypes, either angels or devils, to be worshipped or despised. There are relatively few female characters in the novel — only Miss Havisham, Estella, Mrs Joe and Biddy are significant — whereas there are nine significant male characters.

Of these four female characters, two die, arguably because they have failed to know their place, to be sufficiently passive, subservient or maternal in accordance with social expectations. Miss Havisham is punished for wanting revenge on men and for not settling down to be a maiden aunt in the bosom of her relatives, and Mrs Joe for not curbing her tongue and being too shrewish to her husband and his employees. There is reader sympathy only for Biddy, for whom Pip has no respect until too late; she conforms to conventional womanhood by becoming a good wife and mother, including to Joe whom she teaches to write.

Miss Havisham is punished for wanting revenge on men

It is noticeable in Dickens's novels that the approved female characters are not given comic turns of phrase or regional accents that betray their social class, though their male equivalents are, as in the case of Biddy and Joe who both grew up in the same village. The standards for women are thus perceived to be higher than for men, and women must conform to an ideal of womanhood which includes being well spoken.

New historicism

The approach of this critique is to study the wider cultural, political, social and economic framework of a work of literature to determine the moral values of the author and its characters. In this novel it can be seen that wealth and success in business are a kind of holy grail for everyone, because money and status confer choice and power. Jaggers is a good example of these values in that he is able to state his terms and interfere in the lives of others.

Pip's fantasies shape the development of self and are entirely dictated by the social imperatives of the period, which include the town versus country dialectic. Financial success and class mobility cannot be found in villages, so social aspiration requires a move to at least the county town, and if this is too parochial, then to the great capital itself. London plays a significant role in Pip's formation, just as it dominated the economic traffic of Victorian England and, indeed, large parts of the globe.

Post-structuralism

A post-structuralist reading of the novel would claim that it has no definitive meaning and that no final resolution was possible because of the contradictory impulses of the author and the inherent contradictions in the work, the primary one being the irreconcilability of being both rich and good. A plurality of meanings is generated by adherence to different codes, in this case the pursuit of wealth versus human decency and the imperative to be a good son even though one has not had a good father.

Pip is to be admired for wanting to better himself, as is made clear by the context he wishes to escape from, but he is also criticised by Biddy, and by implication Dickens, for being a snob when he achieves his goal. He is to be pitied when he has no expectations, but either mocked or patronised by others when he has. When he gets into debt we are asked to see this as a moral failure, even though Jaggers predicts it as a foregone conclusion and therefore inevitable.

A satisfactory resolution in terms of the romance genre would be for him to gain and marry Estella, having proved himself worthy of her, but this cannot be allowed because of the didactic nature of the work. As Orwell points out, Dickens 'is always preaching a sermon', and the message of this one is that Pip and Estella have both been damaged as children by selfish adults, so it follows that they are victims of society who will never be able to have children of their own or lead normal family lives. Thus the novel is fundamentally a tragedy and yet it has been adulterated by the structures and devices of comedy to the extent that it cannot be categorised as either genre.

> He is to be pitied when he has no expectations, but either mocked or patronised by others when he has.

Working with the text

Meeting the Assessment Objectives

The four key English literature Assessment Objectives (AOs) describe the different skills you need to show in order to get a good grade. Regardless of what texts or what examination specification you are following, the AOs lie at the heart of your study of English literature at AS and A2; they let you know exactly what the examiners are looking for and provide a helpful framework for your literary studies.

The Assessment Objectives require you to:

- articulate creative, informed and relevant responses to literary texts, using appropriate terminology and concepts, and coherent, accurate written expression **(AO1)**
- demonstrate detailed critical understanding in analysing the ways in which structure, form and language shape meanings in literary texts **(AO2)**
- explore connections and comparisons between different literary texts, informed by interpretations of other readers **(AO3)**
- demonstrate understanding of the significance and influence of the contexts in which literary texts are written and understood **(AO4)**

Try to bear in mind that the AOs are there to support rather than restrict you; do not look at them as encouraging a tick-box approach or a mechanistic, reductive way into the study of literature. Examination questions are written with the AOs in mind, so if you answer them clearly and carefully you should automatically hit the right targets. If you are devising your own questions for coursework, seek the help of your teacher to ensure that your essay title is carefully worded to liberate the required AOs so that you can do your best.

Although the AOs are common to all the exam boards, each specification varies enormously in the way it meets the requirements. The boards' websites provide useful information, including sections for students, past papers, sample papers and mark schemes.

- **AQA**: www.aqa.org.uk
- **Edexcel**: www.edexcel.com
- **OCR**: www.ocr.org.uk
- **WJEC**: www.wjec.co.uk

Remember, though, that your knowledge and understanding of the text still lie at the heart of A-level study, as they always have done. While what constitutes a text may vary according to the specification you are following (e.g. it could be an article, extract, letter, diary, critical essay, review, novel, play or poem), and there may be an emphasis on the different ways texts can be interpreted and considered in relation to different contexts, in the end the study of literature starts with, and comes back to, your engagement with the text itself.

Working with AO1

AO1 focuses upon literary and critical insight, organisation of material and clarity of written communication. Examiners are looking for accurate spelling and grammar, and clarity of thought and expression, so say what you want to say and say it as clearly as you can. Aim for cohesion; your ideas should be presented coherently with an overall sense of a developing argument. Think carefully about your introduction, because your opening paragraph not only sets the agenda for your response but provides the reader with a strong first impression of you — positive or negative. Try to use 'appropriate terminology' but do not hide behind fancy critical terms or complicated language you do not fully understand. 'Feature-spotting' and merely listing literary terms is a classic banana skin all examiners are familiar with.

Choose your references carefully; copying out great gobbets of a text learned by heart underlines your inability to select the choicest short quotation with which to clinch your argument. Regurgitating chunks of material printed on the examination paper without detailed critical analysis is — for obvious reasons — a waste of time; instead try to incorporate brief quotations into your own sentences, weaving them in seamlessly to illustrate your points and develop your argument. The hallmarks of a well written essay — whether for coursework or in an exam — include a clear and coherent introduction that orientates the reader, a systematic and logical argument, aptly chosen and neatly embedded quotations and a conclusion that consolidates your case.

Working with AO2

In studying a text you should think about its overall form (novel, sonnet, tragedy, farce, etc.), structure (how it is organised, how its constituent parts connect with each other) and language. In studying a long novel it might be better to begin with the larger elements of form and structure before considering language. If 'form is meaning', what are the implications of the writer's decision to select this specific genre? Why has the writer chosen to structure the text in the way that they have? In terms of language features, what is most striking about the diction of your text — dialogue, dialect, imagery or symbolism?

In order to discuss language in detail you will need to quote from the text — but the mere act of quoting is not enough to meet AO2. What is important is what you do with the quotation — how you analyse it and how it illuminates your argument. Moreover, since you will often need to make points about larger generic and organisational features such as settings and scenes, which are usually much too long to quote, being able to reference effectively is just as important as mastering the art of the embedded quotation.

Working with AO3

AO3 is a double Assessment Objective that asks you to 'explore connections and comparisons' between texts as well as showing your understanding of the views and interpretations of other**s**. You will find it easier to make comparisons and connections between texts (of any kind) if you try to balance them as you write; remember also that connections and comparisons are not only about finding similarities — differences are just as interesting. Above all, consider how the comparison illuminates each text. It is not just a matter of finding the relationships and connections but of analysing what they show. When writing comparatively, you should use words and constructions that will help you to link your texts, such as 'whereas', 'on the other hand', 'while', 'in contrast', 'by comparison', 'as in', 'differently', 'similarly', 'comparably'.

To access the second half of AO3 effectively you need to measure your own interpretation of a text against those of your teacher and other students. By all means refer to named critics and quote from them if

it seems appropriate, but the examiners are most interested in your personal and creative response. If your teacher takes a particular critical line, be prepared to challenge and question it; there is nothing more dispiriting for an examiner than to read a set of scripts from one centre which all say exactly the same thing. Top candidates produce fresh personal responses rather than merely regurgitating the ideas of others, however famous or insightful their interpretations may be.

Of course your interpretation will only be convincing if it is supported by clear reference to the text and you will only be able to evaluate other readers' ideas if you test them against the evidence of the text itself. AO3 means more than quoting someone else's point of view and saying you agree, although it can be very helpful to use critical views if they push forward an argument of your own and you can offer relevant textual support. Look for other ways of reading texts — from a Marxist, feminist, New historicist, post-structuralist, psychoanalytic, dominant or oppositional point of view — which are more creative and original than merely copying out the ideas of just one person.

Try to show an awareness of multiple readings with regard to your text and an understanding that the meaning of a text is dependent as much upon what the reader brings to it as what the writer left there. Using modal verb phrases such as 'may be seen as', 'might be interpreted as' or 'could be represented as' implies that you are aware that different readers interpret texts in different ways at different times. The key word here is plurality; there is no single meaning, no right answer and you need to evaluate a range of other ways of making textual meanings as you work towards your own.

Working with AO4

AO4, with its emphasis on the 'significance and influence' of the 'contexts in which literary texts are written and received', might at first seem less deeply rooted in the text itself but in fact you are considering and evaluating here the relationship between the text and its contexts. Note the word 'received': this refers to the way interpretation can be influenced by the specific contexts within which the reader is operating; when you are studying a text written many years ago, there is often an immense gulf between its original contemporary context of production and the twenty-first century context in which you receive it.

To access AO4 successfully you need to think about how contexts of production, reception, literature, culture, biography, geography, society, history, genre and intertextuality can affect texts. Place the text at the heart of the web of contextual factors that you feel have had the most impact upon it; examiners want to see a sense of contextual alertness woven seamlessly into the fabric of your essay rather than a clumsy bolted-on rehash of a website or your old history notes. Try to convey your awareness of the fact that literary works contain embedded and encoded representations of the cultural, moral, religious, racial and political values of the society from which they emerged, and that over time attitudes and ideas change until the views they reflect are no longer widely shared. There must be an overlap between a focus on interpretations (AO3) and a focus on contexts, so do not worry about pigeonholing the AOs here.

Taking it ▶
Further ▶

For general advice on writing essays, see the 'Revision advice' on the free website for *Great Expectations* at www. philipallan.co.uk/ literatureguidesonline.

Approaching your written response

You may be studying *Great Expectations* as an examination text or for coursework. Examples are provided here of differnet kinds of question you may be asked that require different types of response.

Examination essay questions

Whole-text essay questions

1 **How has the reader been prepared for the revelation in Chapter 39?**

2 **Illustrate Dickens's power of vivid characterisation by examining the presentation of two of the following characters: Joe, Mrs Joe, Mr Pumblechook, Miss Havisham, Estella, Herbert Pocket.**

3 **'Dickens never departs from his duty of teaching a moral lesson.' Is this the reader's main experience of the novel?**

4 **'*Great Expectations* is characterised by agonised doubt and a profound awareness of social ills.' Do you agree?**

5 **Discuss Dickens's use of humour in *Great Expectations* and its effect on the reader, with reference to three incidents.**

6 **Give two examples of symbolism in *Great Expectations* and show what they contribute to the effect of the novel.**

7 **Give two examples of coincidence in the development of the plot and indicate for what reasons you consider them to be effective or not.**

8 **Select an event in the novel and show how the author has presented it effectively.**

9 'In *Great Expectations* all the characters get what they deserve.' With reference to three characters, say whether you agree.

10 Write an account of the scene in which Magwitch tells Pip that his comfortable life derives from the convict's efforts and summarise Pip's thoughts and feelings which lead him to describe himself as 'wrecked'.

11 'Pathos of the graver and subtler kind is the distinguishing note of *Great Expectations*.' Do you agree with this statement?

12 How realistic do you consider the dialogue of *Great Expectations* to be? Discuss with reference to two or three conversations.

13 How does Dickens develop, in the first 19 chapters, the contrast between the world of the forge and the world of Satis House?

14 Do you agree that the first stage of the novel is more memorable than the other two and, if so, to what do you attribute this?

15 Do you agree that *Great Expectations* is simply a 'snob's progress'?

16 'Rotten architecture, wonderful gargoyles.' Do you agree that the strength of *Great Expectations* lies in detail rather than structure?

17 'What secrecy there is in the young under terror.' Analyse two incidents where Pip is terrified and explain the effect his fear has on his behaviour.

18 What do you consider to be the turning point in Pip's life? Give an account of the incident, making clear the nature of Pip's feelings and what these demonstrate.

19 How does Pip retain reader sympathy in the middle section of the novel, when he is living in London and getting into debt?

20 Pip grows up during the course of the novel. What has he learned and how has he changed by the end?

Extract-based essay questions

Sample question 1

(a) How does the narrative develop in Chapter 18?

(b) How far do you think that *Great Expectations* is a condemnation of wealth?

Possible content for part (a)

- how drama, suspense and mystery have been created by the arrival of the sinister stranger in the village inn, which should be a safe, convivial place
- use of voices and their contrast; effect of use of dialogue; double narrative perspective of younger and older Pip
- importance of setting and atmosphere; social realism of village life
- role of imagery and theme of murder and tragedy
- use of descriptive detail for comedy and threat; humorous devices; theatrical devices; caricature
- this is the turning point for Pip the blacksmith's apprentice; how does he react to idea of becoming a man of means?
- end of a pastoral era; intrusion of corrupt London world; the life of the forge is lost — or is it a blessed release for Pip, as village life was no better, with its jealousies and bullying and lack of hope?
- comment on Joe's reaction and how it differs from Pip's, and how Joe contrasts with Jaggers
- role and significance of characters of Wopsle and Jaggers in novel as a whole

Possible content for part (b)

- moral ambiguity of Pip being rewarded for an act of theft as a child, one provoked by fear more than sympathy
- moral ambiguity of Magwitch being a victim of privileged society and yet his money is tainted — and is rejected ultimately by Pip — because he was a criminal, even though he made his money honestly
- Pip must go abroad and work hard to earn his living and promotion before he can be rehabilitated into society and earn the reader's approbation
- comment on Pip's decline into debt and indolence once in London, and how wealth has changed him
- some wealthy characters are heartless, like Miss Havisham, Estella and Drummle, but Herbert Pocket and Wemmick represent Londoners of the professional class and their materialism, and they are not condemned
- Joe and Biddy have no money, or interest in money, and are the moral heroes of the novel, with simple, homely Christian virtues
- upbringing is a crucial factor: Estella was not born into wealth, but was indoctrinated by Miss Havisham into valuing jewellery and the power of being a lady and having money
- conclusion: that what matters is how one treats other people and that wealth is irrelevant to being a decent and sympathetic human being

Sample question 2

(a) How does the narrative develop in Chapter 49?

(b) What do you think about the view that *Great Expectations* is a Gothic melodrama?

Possible content for part (a)

- this chapter is the climax of Pip's relationship with Miss Havisham and his visits to Satis House; one of a series of visits to the house and journeys between London and Kent which structure the novel and the stages of Pip's development
- reader prepared by gloomy imagery at start: organ, funeral, rooks, grey tower, bare trees — life is empty without Estella; Pip contemplates the ashes of his former hopes
- striking change in Miss Havisham, who is now fearful and wants to be forgiven; is she turning from a 'flat' to a 'round' character, capable of evoking reader sympathy?
- important change in Pip, who is thinking altruistically of Herbert (and Estella) and wants nothing for himself; he is capable of forgiveness which is part of his moral regeneration
- key chapter in the detective mystery strand of the novel, as Pip now knows more than Miss Havisham (Estella's mother's identity); Pip is no longer dependent on her and is in charge of the dialogue
- vision of body in the twilight one of a series of structural references to illusions and hangings, and a presentiment creating tension
- fire has been a recurring image and now it becomes a significant plot element
- Pip's fight with the burning body is reminiscent of many others in the novel, particularly that between the convicts on the marshes: 'struggling like desperate enemies'; 'like a prisoner who might escape'
- ironic because he is trying to save her not destroy her; ironic that he should wish to do so; ironic that she should catch fire because of being upset about Pip and Estella
- chapter ends, like others, with the written word; writing and being able to write are motifs in the novel

Possible content for part (b)

- novel is many things: *Bildungsroman*, romance, thriller, mystery, social comedy — but it is also melodramatic and full of theatrical devices
- characters all exaggerated in their mannerisms and philosophies — e.g. catchphrases and extreme appearance — and Pip is peculiarly sensitive and 'romantic', dwelling on his feelings and obsession with Estella

- many characters recognisable as fairytale stereotypes, e.g. Mrs Joe the wicked stepmother, Miss Havisham the witch, Estella the spoilt princess in her castle
- language is often highly charged and emotive, using pathos (as in Chapter 49 with the anguished repetition of 'What have I done! What have I done!')
- many confrontations in the novel — which largely rely on coincidence — and most of them involve some form of violence
- Gothic horror devices of split personalities, love triangles, promises and prophecies coming true (as in Chapter 49) are employed
- many of the settings are ruins or buildings in a state of decay — including the graveyard and prison — or full of black or sinister objects, such as Jaggers's office and home; scene in Chapter 49 like a stage set with the 'ragged chair' and the fireplace at the centre; Miss Havisham in the grotesque costume of the decaying bridal dress
- recurring imagery of moths, death, murder, Shakespeare's Gothic tragedies (*Macbeth* and *Hamlet*) and link with *Frankenstein*: Pip and Estella are Miss Havisham's experiment which has gone wrong
- key events take place in darkness or storms and a fearful atmosphere is evoked; shadows and hallucinations, ghosts and disguises, shrieks and moans are used for dramatic visual and acoustic effect
- many deaths and death threats in the novel, all spectacular, and strong revenge theme driven by Orlick, a stage villain with no redeeming qualities
- however, Gothic and melodramatic features balanced by softer elements: comic interludes; a sort of resolution at the end (mention the two endings); moral growth of Pip; peacefulness of Magwitch's end; the goodness of Joe and Biddy; the next generation in the form of Little Pip

Comparative essay questions

1 'It is essential for a novelist to make the reader care about the main character and the way that s/he develops.' How far do you agree with this statement? In your response, you should comment on and analyse the connections and comparisons between *at least two* texts you have studied.

2 'What makes a main character interesting is their flaws, rather than their perfections, for the reader can only identify with someone they recognise as human.' How far do you agree with this statement? In your response, you should comment on and analyse the connections and comparisons between *at least two* texts you have studied.

3 Show how the main character learns through experience and making mistakes in the course of *at least two* texts you have studied.

Coursework

Great Expectations is a novel that may be selected as a coursework text for several examination boards. Coursework tasks can be of two kinds:

- critical or explorative study (often comparative)
- re-creative piece or creative response

Sample coursework titles for critical/explorative study

1 '*Great Expectations* emphasises human subjection to time.' Explore the ways in which this is conveyed in the novel.

2 Examine the role played by wealth in *Great Expectations*.

3 Outline the part played in the novel by Estella, making clear Pip's attitude towards her, and hers to him, how she uses and is used by others, and contrasting her character with that of Biddy.

Sample re-creative coursework titles

1 Imagine that you are Pip at the end of the novel. Make a speech to little Pip explaining why you went away, and why you came back, and tell him what you think he should know about the past. Adopt a suitable voice and style.

2 Imagine that you are Estella at the end of the novel. Write a letter to Pip in which you tell him what you feel towards him and Miss Havisham now, and about your life as the wife of Drummle. Adopt a suitable voice and style.

3 You are Miss Havisham after the fire. Reflect upon your life and describe your thoughts and feelings about Pip. You may wish to include references to Estella, Jaggers, Compeyson and the Pockets. Adopt a suitable voice and style.

4 You are Magwitch at the point of death. Reflect upon your life and describe your thoughts and feelings about Pip. You may wish to include references to Estella, Molly, Jaggers and Compeyson. Adopt a suitable voice and style.

Three sample essays and an extended commentary can be found in the online resources that accompany this book.

Top ten quotations

I always treated him as a larger species of child... (p. 9, Chapter 2)

1

In Dickens children represent innocence and goodness, in the Romantic tradition, until if and when they are corrupted by guilt in the form of an adult demand. Joe is still a child, motivated by a general benevolence and free of all resentment. Even the very young Pip appreciates that he is different from all the other adults he knows.

...her light came along the dark passage like a star. (p. 59, Chapter 8)

2

Estella, in the context of the darkness of Satis House, is immediately equated with light and is the bearer of the glimmer of aspiration into Pip's mundane and lowly life. She is a star out of his sphere, however, and not destined to be his.

And the mists had all solemnly risen now, and the world lay spread before me. (p. 160, Chapter 19)

3

This ending to Volume I is one of the many references to mist in the novel, its rising always symbolising a clarity of vision and hopefulness. This is ironic here, however, as the world of London may be spread before Pip, but it will not bring him the success or happiness he expects and craves.

...do all the shining deeds of the young Knight of romance, and marry the Princess. (p. 231, Chapter 29)

4

Pip the romantic dreamer chooses to believe that he and Estella are fairytale characters and that Miss Havisham is their fairy godmother. This is painfully far from the truth, in all three cases. They are all tainted by criminality and are more creatures of the Gothic horror genre than of a story which will end happily ever after.

The figure of my sister in her chair by the kitchen fire, haunted me night and day. (p. 278, Chapter 35)

5

This is just one of the many references to haunting in the novel. Pip's macabre imagination makes him susceptible to the idea of ghosts. Although Pip feels no tenderness towards his sister's memory, he is still shocked by her death and feels he should wish to avenge it. This is one of many links with the plot and the sentiments of *Hamlet*.

6

> The abhorrence in which I held the man, the dread I had of him, the repugnance with which I shrank from him, could not have been exceeded if he had been some terrible beast. (pp. 319–20, Chapter 39)

This is an example of several aspects of the novel in one sentence: irony in that this is how Pip repays his benefactor, rather than with the expected gratitude, and that Magwitch should have waited for and imagined this moment for so many years; the use of a triple structure to convey strength of feeling; a reference to the horror genre in the idea of a 'terrible beast'. Pip is alone in his rooms on a dark night, and at the mercy of a convict and possible murderer, and the reader is in suspense as to what he might do to Pip, especially if he notices Pip's revulsion.

7

> O, that he had never come! That he had left me at the forge — far from contented, yet, by comparison, happy! (p. 321, Chapter 39)

This is Pip's first reaction to the arrival and revelation of his benefactor. It can be interpreted as ingratitude, or as an indication of how completely devastated Pip is by the knowledge that he has been living on tainted money, when he has wished so devoutly to distance himself from what he perceives to be his guilty past.

8

> ...I could never, never, never, undo what I had done. (p. 323, Chapter 39)

For Pip the advent of Magwitch has caused a moment of anagnorisis (a character's recognition of a revealing truth) — he suddenly realises how worthless his behaviour to the simple and faithful Joe and Biddy has been. This triple usage of an absolute echoes Macbeth's 'What's done cannot be undone.' It draws attention to the tragic helplessness of erring humans who cannot right their wrongs however much they wish it, and who must live with the consequences.

9

> ...when I took my place by Magwitch's side, I felt that that was my place henceforth while he lived. (p. 446, Chapter 54)

This is a key moment for Pip of renunciation of worldly and selfish pursuits and a recognition of his moral duty towards his benefactor, and thereby his own salvation.

10

> I took her hand in mine, and we went out of the ruined place; and, as the morning mists had risen long ago when I first left the forge, so, the evening mists were rising now, and in all the broad expanse of tranquil light they showed

to me, I saw the shadow of no parting from her. (p. 484, Chapter 59)

This poignant final sentence of the changed ending has the positive language of hand-holding and the rising of mist, as well as the absence of shadows which have dogged Pip throughout the novel. This is as near as Dickens is willing to get to saying that Pip and Estella are now united, rising like the phoenix from the ashes of Satis House.

Taking it further

Books

- Brooks, P. (1984) *Reading for the Plot: Design and Intention in Narrative*, Oxford University Press.
  - Contains the essay 'Repetition, Repression and Return: *Great Expectations* and the Study of Plot'.
- Carey, J. (1991) *The Violent Effigy: A Study of Dickens's Imagination*, Faber & Faber.
  - A perceptive study of how Dickens's imagination colours his novels.
- Gilmour, R. (1981) *The Idea of the Gentleman in the Victorian Novel*, Routledge.
  - Contains a long chapter on *Great Expectations*.
- Leavis, F. R. and Leavis, Q. D. (1970) *Dickens the Novelist*, Chatto & Windus.
  - Contains the essay 'How we must read *Great Expectations*'.
- Orwell, G. (1968) *Essays, Journalism and Letters of George Orwell, Vol. 1*, Secker & Warburg.
  - Contains the essay 'Charles Dickens'.
- Page, N. (1979) (ed.) *Hard Times, Great Expectations and Our Mutual Friend: A Casebook*, Macmillan.
- Price, M. (1987) (ed.) *Charles Dickens: Twentieth Century Views*, Prentice-Hall.
  - Contains a useful essay by Paul Pickrel on *Great Expectations*.
- Sell, R. D. (1994) (ed.) *Great Expectations: A New Casebook*, Macmillan.

Articles from *The English Review*

- Holford, M., 'Doubling in *Great Expectations*: A sixth-form view', *The English Review*, Vol. 4, No. 2.
- Buckland, A., 'Great speculations: Charles Dickens and nineteenth-century science', *The English Review*, Vol. 17, No. 3.

Film/television productions

All of the productions listed below are available on DVD.

- 1946 — starring Jean Simmons and John Mills, directed by David Lean; a classic and stylish production
- 1974 — starring Sarah Miles and Michael York, directed by Joseph Hardy; viewed as a rather undistinguished production
- 1981 — BBC production starring Sarah-Jane Varley and Gerry Sundquist, directed by Julian Amyes; a typical high-quality BBC production of the period
- 1989 — Disney production starring Kim Thomson, Anthony Calf and Anthony Hopkins, directed by Kevin Connor; a classic American production
- 1998 — updated version starring Ethan Hawke and Gwyneth Paltrow, directed by Alfonso Cuarón; set in modern-day New York — Finn, a painter, pursues his unrequited and haughty childhood sweetheart, Estella
- 1999 — BBC production starring Justine Waddell and Ioan Gruffudd, directed by Julian Jarrold; arguably the best filmed version of the novel

Scenes from several of these may be found on **www.youtube.com**

Internet resources

A Google search for 'Great Expectations' returns over seven million results. It would be more than a lifetime's work to go through all these. What follows is a selection of sites that are useful and seem to have broadly reliable information.

The best site for *Great Expectations* is the Victorian Web at

- **www.victorianweb.org/authors/dickens/ge/geov.html**

This includes a biography, a large quantity of background material and dozens of critical essays.

The full text of the novel is available online at a number of sites; two easily accessible ones are:

- http://etext.virginia.edu/toc/modeng/public/DicGrea.html
- www.gutenberg.org/etext/1400

There are several free online study guides, including:

- www.shmoop.com/great-expectations/
  Written by postgraduates from top US universities.

The following site is an extensive portal for Dickens and all his works:

- http://www.lang.nagoya-u.ac.jp/~matsuoka/Dickens.html